U.S.S. CONSTITUTION

1817

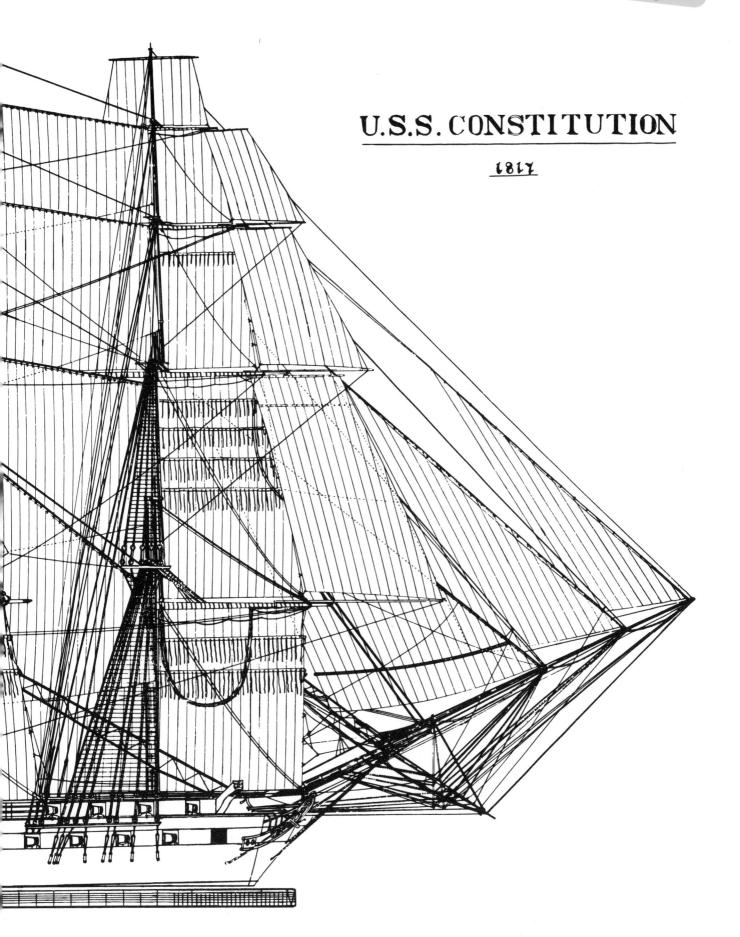

OLD IRONSIDES

OLD IRONSIDES

An Illustrated History of *USS Constitution*

Thomas P. Horgan
Captain, USNR (Ret.)

YANKEE BOOKS
Camden, Maine

Table of Contents

Acknowledgements

So much has been written about the career of the nation's most famous warship, U.S.S. *Constitution,* that inevitably conflicts and disagreements have intruded. This volume is an effort to present a concise and reliable version. Much of Old Ironsides' story has filtered down through the years with scant documentation, and the most challenging phase of this task has been to separate fact from fiction. In striving for this objective, unstinting assistance and encouragement from many sources are gratefully acknowledged. We particularly wish to thank:

Rear Admiral Ernest M. Eller, director of naval history and curator for the Navy Department, for reviewing the original manuscript.

Rear Admiral Joseph H. Wellings, commandant of the First Naval District at the inception of this volume, who furnished valued advice and support.

Commander George M. Hall, former public information officer of the First Naval District, for his able assistance and encouragement, from the origin of the idea through the completion of the book.

The Boston Naval Shipyard, the Navy's Office of Information, the First Naval District's Public Information Office, the Office of Naval History, the Library of Congress, the U.S.S. *Constitution* Museum, and the National Park Service.

A period of nearly twenty years has spanned the time between the inception of the book in the early 1960's and the printing of this updated edition in 1980. During this time, *Constitution* has had several commanding officers, and it has been our pleasure to work directly with three of them: Lieutenant Victor B. Stevens, Commander John D. McKinnon, and Commander Robert L. Gillen.

Foreword

My earliest memories of the United States Navy go back to the days when, as a small boy, I used to be taken to the U.S.S. *Constitution* in Charlestown, Massachusetts. The sight of that historic frigate, with its tall spars and black guns, stirred my imagination and made American history come alive for me. I know that a visit to Old Ironsides has done the same for many thousands of young Americans. I am glad that Captain Horgan has now set down the narrative of its incomparable fighting record and of its subsequent vicissitudes.

I am glad too because of the role my own family was privileged to play in its preservation. When the *Constitution* was first inscribed for destruction in 1830, Oliver Wendell Holmes wrote "Old Ironsides" to rouse the nation and save the ship. More than half a century later, my grandfather, Congressman John F. Fitzgerald, found the gallant old ship rotting away in the Portsmouth Navy Yard. In 1897 he submitted a resolution to the House of Representatives calling on the Secretary of the Navy to take steps to save it again. This effort helped keep the *Constitution* afloat until a major job of reconstruction could be carried through in the 1920's. The ship then found its final refuge in Charlestown. Later, as a congressman myself, I was proud that Charlestown — and Old Ironsides — lay within my constituency.

I hope that as many Americans as possible will visit the *Constitution* in years to come, and I hope that those who cannot will read Captain Horgan's book.

John F. Kennedy

Introduction

This edition of *Old Ironsides* will undoubtedly enlighten you, the reader, with the history of America's oldest fighting ship, the U.S.S. *Constitution*. The effort to maintain her in the fine condition that she enjoys today has been a result of the concentrated efforts of many individuals throughout her long and illustrious 190-year career.

On December 17, 1987, I had the distinct honor to accept — on behalf of the U.S. Navy, the crew of "Old Ironsides," and all those who have contributed to her preservation through the years — the prestigious World Ship Trust Award. This international award is presented by heads of state to ships which exemplify outstanding maritime preservation. It was indeed fitting and a significant milestone in the grand history of "Old Ironsides" that this award was presented during the year of the bicentennial of the U.S. Constitution, the document for which President Washington named the ship.

The World Ship Trust Award was presented by President Reagan in the Oval Office. The inscription reads:

> Presented on behalf of the World Ship Trust by the President of the United States to the United States Navy in grateful recognition of its genius and enterprise in preserving and exhibiting the U.S. Frigate *Constitution,* "Old Ironsides," of 1797, thereby splendidly enriching the maritime heritage of all mankind — 1987

This edition of Thomas P. Horgan's outstanding book will, I'm certain, provide you with a great deal of pleasure and insight into our national maritime heritage, most particularly to the successes and travails of the oldest fighting ship afloat and in commission in the world.

As you enjoy this book, please remember that it has been through the dedicated efforts of many people that "Old Ironsides" has been maintained so long and so well. This book salutes those Americans who have worked so diligently to preserve the memory of our great maritime and naval history. Most important is the contribution of the hundreds of thousands who show their interest and appreciation each year by visiting the U.S.S. *Constitution* in Charlestown, Massachusetts.

The U.S.S. *Constitution* serves to remind us that each generation of Americans has risen and must continue to rise to the challenge of defending our freedoms. I am certain you will enjoy reading Captain Horgan's superb account of the history of "Old Ironsides." It is a book that can be enjoyed many times over and it will serve to inspire or renew the moving experience of walking the decks of "Old Ironsides." I extend to everyone an invitation to visit the U.S.S. *Constitution* and experience firsthand the living history of our Navy and maritime heritage of this great nation.

D. M. Cashman
Commander, U.S. Navy

62nd in Command
U.S.S. *Constitution*

OLD IRONSIDES

Ay, tear her tattered ensign down!
　Long has it waved on high,
And many an eye has danced to see
　That banner in the sky;
Beneath it rung the battle shout,
　And burst the cannon's roar; —
The meteor of the ocean air
　Shall sweep the clouds no more!

Her deck, once red with heroes' blood,
　Where knelt the vanquished foe,
When winds were hurrying o'er the flood,
　And waves were white below,
No more shall feel the victor's tread,
　Or know the conquered knee; —
The harpies of the shore shall pluck
　The eagle of the sea!

Oh, better that her shattered hulk
　Should sink beneath the wave;
Her thunders shook the mighty deep,
　And there should be her grave;
Nail to the mast her holy flag,
　Set every threadbare sail,
And give her to the god of storms,
　The lightning and the gale!

Oliver Wendell Holmes, 1830

OLD IRONSIDES

PART I

An Illustrated History

A New Nation

No warship that ever sailed the seas better served her country than "Old Ironsides," U.S.S. *Constitution.*

She brought dignity to an infant nation and won the respect and admiration of great world powers — although she often had only grudging support from the country she defended.

She had something more important: the unstinting devotion of a small company of brave men, spirited volunteers, whose seamanship and gunnery never failed to defeat her foes. Service with *Constitution* produced many of the nation's outstanding naval leaders.

The frigate was planned and constructed for speed that would enable her to escape any opponent she could not defeat. Her record proves the soundness of this concept, and *Constitution* remains a symbol of the nation's sea power to this day.

After the Revolutionary War, the new United States disbanded its small fleet, wanting only to pursue peaceful commerce on the seas. But the seas were far from peaceful and the nation was powerless to protect her far-ranging merchant vessels. In the Mediterranean, fierce Barbary pirates preyed on merchant ships. American ships also were subject to outrages by both England and France. Great Britain and France were locked in a long and bitter struggle that raged over Europe and the seas. Both countries ignored American rights as a neutral and harassed Yankee shipping with crippling effect. Many American merchants, more concerned with their expanding foreign trade than with their country's honor, wished to avoid war at any cost, and felt the way to do so was to purchase immunity and remain unarmed.

In 1785 the United States had not a single armed vessel and only a small sea force when the North African pirates gave America's merchant marine their undivided attention. European nations had made treaties with the pirates — which made sitting ducks of American shipping, the only prey left to the corsairs. European nations had reason to be pleased with this harassment of a flourishing rival. The ruler of Algiers, the dey, frankly summed up his situation: "If I were to make peace with everybody, what should I do with my corsairs? They would take off my head for the want of other prizes, not being able to live on their miserable allowance."

THE AVENGING EAGLE — *This carved representation of the American eagle is one of four decorating the gangways of Old Ironsides. They well represent the fierce determination of the infant U. S. Navy, which made freedom of the seas a national policy. Old Ironsides remains today a symbol of the nation's sea power — the world's oldest warship in commission afloat.*

The Algerians captured eleven American merchant vessels within a period of a few weeks in 1793, and imprisoned 106 mariners. There had been ample prior provocation for Congress to act, and it finally did so, apparently stirred by a letter from a captive captain and an accompanying petition signed by thirteen American shipmasters. Captain Richard O'Brien asked for immediate steps to protect our merchant fleet and warned Congress that if this were not done the corsairs would control the Atlantic Ocean and be tempted to raid the coastal waters of the United States. The thirteen captains, in pleading for the prisoners, some of whom had endured eight years of hard labor, wrote: "Your petitioners pray you will take their unfortunate situation into consideration, and adopt such measures as will restore the American captives to their country, their friends, families and connections; and your petitioners will ever pray and be thankful."

Even though Congress could no longer tolerate international banditry and appropriated funds for six frigates, including *Constitution,* it had stipulated that construction would be halted if immunity for our merchant ships could be purchased through treaty. Such a treaty was obtained from Algiers in 1795 just as *Constitution* and some of the other frigates were nearing completion, and construction was suspended. Terms of the treaty included payment to the dey of approximately a million dollars in cash, plus the gift of a new frigate and $21,600 in naval stores annually during the life of the treaty. The new frigate named *Crescent* was built at Portsmouth, New Hampshire, at a cost of $100,000. Aboard when she sailed for delivery to the dey of Algiers was Captain O'Brien, returning as Consul General to all the Barbary States, where he had been imprisoned for ten years.

The Christian nations of Europe had bowed to extortion by the North African Moors for three centuries. Together, the maritime nations, particularly England, France, and Holland, easily could have ended plundering operations of the Barbary pirates, but in their trade rivalry they felt it more advantageous to keep the robbers in business as a check on competitors.

The Barbary pirates were not alone in refusing to show respect to our young nation. England and France continued their humiliating and hostile acts against the United States, and President George Washington was not happy with a submissive policy. In 1796 he advised Congress: "It is our experience that the most sincere neutrality is not sufficient guard against the depredations of nations at war. To secure respect to a neutral flag requires a naval force organized and ready to protect it from insult or aggression."

England had long used brutal press gangs to drag her own people from their homes and families to man her fleet. So it was only a short step when they extended this system to the impressment of American merchant seamen, forcing them to serve on British ships. Usually this was done on the pretext they were British subjects.

British and, particularly, French aggression continued, and in July 1797, Congress authorized funds to resume construction of six frigates. *Constitution* was one of the six.

BIRD OF PREY — *This rakish craft was typical of those used by the Barbary pirates in plundering merchant ships. The raiders were fast and were handled skillfully under sail by their fierce crews. They were an elusive foe, for their slight draft often let them escape in waters too shallow for pursuit. Seagoing racketeers, the pirates specialized in robbery, slavery, and the gathering of "protection money."*

Joshua Humphreys's correspondence with Robert Morris, Minister of Finance, may well have won him the assignment to design the six frigates authorized by Congress. Some of his ideas were so sound that they have influenced our naval construction through modern times.

Sir, From the present appearance of affairs I believe it is time this country was possessed of a navy; but as that is yet to be raised, I have ventured a few remarks on the subject.

Ships that compose the European navys are generally distinguished by their rates; but as the situation and depth of water of our coasts and harbors are different in some degrees from those in Europe, and as our navy for a considerable time will be inferior in numbers, we are to consider what size ships will be most formidable, and be an overmatch for those of an enemy; such frigates as in blowing weather would be an overmatch for double-deck ships, and in light winds to evade coming to action; or double-deck ships that would be an overmatch for common double-deck ships, and in blowing weather superior to ships of three decks, or in calm weather or light winds to outsail them. Ships built on these principles will render those of an enemy in a degree useless, or require a greater number before they dare attack our ships. . . . As such ships will cost a large sum of money, they should be built of the best materials that could possibly be procured. . . .

The greatest care should be taken in the construction of such ships . . . for if we should be obliged to take a part in the present European war, or at a future day we should be dragged into a war with any powers of the Old Continent, especially Great Britain, they having such a number of ships of that size . . . it would be an equal chance by equal combat that we lose our ships. . . . Several questions will arise, whether one large or two small frigates contribute most to the protection of our trade, or which will cost the least sum of money, or whether two small ones are as able to engage a double-deck ship as one large one. For my part I am decidedly of opinion the large ones will answer best.

Joshua Humphreys

Sir,

W O. July 7ᵗʰ 1797

It being necessary to fix on a Name for the Frigate intended for the Dey of Algiers before she sails from Portsmouth: I have therefore concluded to call her the Crescent, which Name you will be pleased to have inserted in her papers and other documents —

I have just received your favor of the 29 ᵗʰ Ultᵒ and I congratulate you and Mr Hackett on the safe Launching of the Frigate into her proper element —

A BITTER TASK — *The shipwrights of Portsmouth, New Hampshire who built a fine frigate for the dey of Algiers in 1797 had little reason to enjoy their labor. The new warship had been exacted under terms of a treaty that sought to purchase immunity for American merchantmen from Algerian corsairs. The frigate, called* Crescent, *after the emblem much used by the Moors, was laden with other tribute and delivered the next year. Apparently, no one recognized in the transaction the arming of a bandit. The Secretary of War was forced to handle the humiliating affair with the best possible grace — as seen in the accompanying letter to the builders. Shipbuilding was handled by the War Office until establishment of the Navy Department in 1798.*

AN EAGLE IN ARMOR — *The American eagle is the national emblem. This fine example of the wood-carver's art graces Old Ironsides' stern. The fearless, feathered warrior reflects the country's early determination to remain free. It was widely used for decoration in sailing-ship days by merchant ships as well as by the Navy. Surviving examples of the almost-lost art have become museum treasures.*

A New Frigate

Constitution was built at Edmund Hartt's shipyard, across Boston Harbor from her permanent berth at the Naval Shipyard. The Coast Guard later established its Boston base at the site. Nearby were Paul Revere's home and the Old North Church.

Although records credit Joshua Humphreys with the basic design of the frigates, he had valuable assistance from others; in particular, Josiah Fox, who was also a skilled naval architect. The two men had something else in common. Both were known as Quakers, and their part in producing ships of war disturbed members of the Society of Friends.

When construction of *Constitution* and five other frigates was authorized on March 27, 1794, most of the necessary timber still stood in the forest. Joshua Humphreys specified that only the best be used, and men were sent to scout the forests to find it. Tall pines were felled at Unity, Maine, dragged and rolled to the sea, and towed to Boston for *Constitution*'s masts. Large quantities of white oak were obtained in the New England area. But it was necessary to search more widely for live oak — so called because its great strength and durability made it the best of all timber for building wooden ships. After scouts located a good supply on a group of islands in Georgia, the government bought three of the islands for $16,000, approximately the value of the live oak needed for the six frigates. Large quantities of yellow pine were brought from Georgia and South Carolina.

Paul Revere, a man of many talents, furnished much of *Constitution*'s copper and composition hardware, using his own formulas. Included were bolts, rods and other fastenings, and copper sheathing for her bottom. He had promised the materials "as cheap as any one," and was paid $3,820.33. Anchors were made at Hanover, Massachusetts.

Construction of *Constitution* could proceed only at the pace at which materials arrived. In those days a shipyard little resembled the highly mechanized establishments we see now. All that was required was a piece of shore property suitable for building and launching ways. A hull was fabricated to a great extent by hand labor, and skilled adzmen made a major contribution. An adz resembles a curved axhead fitted at right angles to the handle. Ship carpenters used them with the care of a sculptor. There were almost no straight lines — curves were virtually the rule in building a wooden hull. Few pieces of timber could be cut to the

A GALA AFFAIR — Constitution*'s launching in 1797 was a festive event that attracted a throng of officials and citizens. In his announcement to the public, the builder spoke of his "conducting into the ocean, a powerful agent of national justice, which hope dictates may become the just pride and ornament of the American name." This faith in* Constitution *soon was justified. The launching site was directly across the harbor from the present Charlestown Navy Yard, where* Constitution *has been berthed during most of the years she has not been at sea.*

TWO CENTURIES LATER — *Boston Harbor today is a far cry from the young seaport that witnessed the launching of* Constitution *in 1797. This elevated view shows the ship's mainmast during the final stages of an overhaul in 1979. (An interesting comparison can be made between this photo and the one on page 122.)*

DOWN THE WAYS — *Fears were expressed that* Constitution's *entry into the harbor might cause a minor tidal wave. The public was cautioned to guard against being swept from nearby wharves, but this warning was unnecessary. Note that the artist has pictured the Old North Church between the fore and mainmasts. From its steeple, Paul Revere received the lantern signal which sent him on his famous ride to alarm the citizenry of the approach of the British in the War of Independence. Revere supplied much of* Constitution's *hardware, including the copper that covers her hull up to the waterline.*

same measure. Shipbuilding had little in common with house carpentry.

In some sections, *Constitution*'s hull was protected by more than twenty inches of frames and planking, the heaviest being near the waterline. In general, she was built as strongly as the major war vessels of the time — the line-of-battle ships. Thousands of wooden treenails were used in place of metal spikes to fasten timbers together. Pronounced "trunnels," they usually were made of locust and were immovable after they were swelled by dampness.

Constitution's designed dimensions gave her a length over all of 204 feet and 175 feet on the load waterline, and a beam of 43 feet, 6 inches; her best sailing draft was 21 feet forward and 23 feet aft. Her tonnage under old measurement rules ranged from 1,335 to 1,576 tons. Many years later, the Navy listed her displacement at 2,200 tons, about the same as some World War II destroyers.

Constitution was provided a suit of thirty-six sails, almost all square and made of flax. They had an area of 42,720 square feet, approximately an acre. The largest unit was the 3,400-square-foot main topsail. Well over two miles of hemp cordage were required for running rigging to manage the sails. This did not include standing rigging used to support the masts or cordage used other places on the ship.

The complexities of this "power plant"

give some idea of the importance of the sailing master, whose responsibility was to handle the ship even during the fury of battle. Records indicate *Constitution*'s top speed was thirteen and a half knots. Many steam vessels never moved so fast.

Construction of *Constitution* was suspended after the signing of a treaty with Algiers, and it was not until July 1797 that Congress appropriated funds to complete the ship. She was launched October 21, 1797, under circumstances likely to make sailors, always superstitious folk, fear she would be a jinx ship. The launching had been attempted a month earlier, but she stuck on the ways. Force was applied, but she moved only about twenty-five feet before stopping dead as the ways settled. A huge crowd of spectators, which included many notables, went home disappointed. Two days later another thirty feet were gained. After the inclination of the ways was steepened, the launch was completed on October 21 on the next favorable tide.

The other five frigates were completed and launched. They were the 44-gun frigates *President* at New York, *United States* at Philadelphia, *Chesapeake* at Norfolk, and 36-gun *Constellation* at Baltimore and *Congress* at Portsmouth. During construction, *Chesapeake* was changed to a 36-gun rating, leaving the ships evenly divided between 44- and 36-gun frigates.

Quasi War

Our Quasi War with France gave *Constitution* her first active duty in 1798. There was little enthusiasm for conflict with a nation that only two decades earlier had been a valued ally in our War of Independence. However, France forced hostilities by persistent raids on our merchant ships, violations of neutrality, and refusal to deal with our diplomats. Congress finally voided all treaties and directed our naval forces to seek out armed French vessels.

Constitution departed Boston on July 22, 1798, less than a year off the launching ways, and was soon bound for the West Indies. She was unsuited to her task, since most of the French vessels in the area were small, swift privateers that could easily elude a heavy frigate in the shallow, dangerous waters of the Indies. The operations served *Constitution* as little more than a training cruise. The cruise did, however, furnish a preview of her sailing qualities and the skill and daring of a young officer, Lieutenant Isaac Hull, who some years later became one of her most famous commanders.

Constitution, commanded by Commodore Silas Talbot, who had recently relieved her first commander, Samuel Nicholson, was patrolling off San Domingo when she encountered the British frigate *Santa Margaretta*. Diplomatically, the two nations were on friendly terms. The British commander, a Captain Parker, was an old acquaintance of Talbot's. The commodore invited him aboard *Constitution*.

The British were contemptuous of the new American frigates, but the visiting captain professed admiration for *Constitution*. This could have been little more than courtesy, because Captain Parker promptly added an opinion that his command could outsail the American ship. Talbot accepted the challenge and a race was arranged for a few weeks later. The stake was a cask of Madeira wine on the challenger's side against its value in cash.

Before the race, the British frigate was

A CHAMPION CUTS HER TEETH — *After her launching,* Constitution *was outfitted for sea under the direction of her commander, Captain Samuel Nicholson. She first sailed in 1798. Her builders' predicted speed soon was tested and the powerful new frigate was not found wanting. On one of her early cruises she met a British frigate off the West Indies whose skipper was an acquaintance of Commodore Silas Talbot, who had succeeded Nicholson to the command of* Constitution. *This was during a period of uneasy peace with England. The Britisher came aboard as a visitor and after inspecting* Constitution *proposed a test of speed. England was given a preview of what she was to later encounter in the War of 1812; the challenger was far astern after a dawn-to-dusk sailing duel.*

A DARING RAID — Constitution *was seeking French privateers in May 1800 when Isaac Hull first displayed the skill and courage that later brought him fame. Commodor Talbot assigned Hull, his first lieutenant, and a party of bluejackets and marines to the sloop* Sally *and sent them to cut out the French privateer* Sandwich. *The French ship had taken refuge in the Spanish harbor of Port Platte, San Domingo. The marines spiked harbor guns as sailors from* Sally *boarded and quickly subdued* Sandwich's *crew. Above, marines are shown landing to spike the guns of the fort while* Sally *draws alongside* Sandwich. *At right, Hull's men take the French privateer. Those who took part in the raid were praised, but the seizure in a neutral port was ruled illegal and the prize returned.*

30

tuned up and her bottom cleaned and she reported for the sailing duel as trim as a racing yacht.

Isaac Hull was made responsible for handling *Constitution.* The starting gun was at dawn; the finish at sunset. The course was directly to windward. The two frigates beat to windward all day, and on square-rigged vessels this meant a tremendous amount of sail handling. Hull lured his opponent into frequent short tacks instead of sailing long ones, confident *Constitution*'s crew would be livelier than the men of *Santa Margaretta.* His reputation for excellence of ship handling, which has never dimmed, was established during this race.

At sunset the British frigate was far astern. When the victor joined the vanquished after dark, Captain Parker was waiting in his gig with the cask of Madeira.

On May 10, 1800, there was another exploit that threw the spotlight on Isaac Hull. Commodore Talbot had discovered a French privateer in the neutral Spanish harbor of Port Platte, San Domingo, West Indies. The incident is best described in Talbot's report to the Secretary of the Navy.

> I have now to acquaint you, Sir, that I have for some time been meditating an enterprise against a French armed ship lying at Port Platte, protected by her own guns and a fort of three heavy cannon. It was my first intention to have gone in with the *Constitution,* and to have silenced the fort and ship, which has all her guns on one side, to cooperate with the fort in defending against any hostile force; but after the best information I could gain, I found it to be somewhat dangerous to approach the entrance of the harbor, with a ship of the draft of water of the *Constitution.*
>
> Having detained the sloop *Sally*... I conceived that this sloop would be a suitable vessel for a disguise. I, therefore, manned her at sea from the *Constitution,* with about ninety brave seamen and marines, the latter to be commanded by Captain Carmick and Lieutenant Armory, when on shore; but the entire command I gave to Mr. Isaac Hull, my first lieutenant, who entered the harbor of Port Platte yesterday in open day, with his men in

the hold of the sloop, except five or six to work her in. They ran alongside of the ship, and boarded her sword in hand, without the loss of a man, killed or wounded. At the moment the ship was boarded, agreeably to my plan, Captain Carmick and Lieutenant Amory landed with the marines, up to their necks in water, and spiked all the cannon in the fort, before the commanding officer had time to recollect and prepare himself for defense.

> Perhaps no enterprise of the same moment was ever better executed; and I feel myself under great obligations to Lieutenant Hull, Captain Carmick and Lieutenant Amory, for their avidity in undertaking the scheme I had planned, and for the handsome manner and great address with which they performed this daring venture.
>
> The ship, I understand, mounts four sixes and two nines; she was formerly the British packet *Sandwich,* and from the boasting publications ... and the declaration of the officers, she is one of the fastest sailors that swims. She ran three or four years (if I forget not), as a privateer out of France, and with greater success than any other that ever sailed out of their ports. She is a beautiful copper bottomed ship; her cargo consists principally of sugar and coffee.

The capture, however, put no sugar in the coffee of *Constitution*'s crew. Our government acknowledged that the seizure in a neutral port was illegal and *Sandwich* was returned, together with damages met, in part at least, by prize money due *Constitution*'s crew from other captures.

This did not prevent the Secretary of the Navy from complimenting Commodore Talbot for "protecting with effect a great proportion of our commerce, in laying the foundation of a permanent trade with San Domingo, and in causing the American character to be respected."

A treaty ended hostilities with France in March 1801, and Congress put the Navy on peacetime status, although outrages by the Barbary pirates continued. *Constitution* was retired and spent two decommissioned years at the Boston Navy Yard. Then she embarked on her most glorious years by sailing against the corsairs.

INTO THE PIRATES' LAIR — *The worst reverse in the war with Tripoli took place when the corsairs captured* Philadelphia, *for with her went a major part of Commodore Edward Preble's firepower. The loss of the 36-gun frigate was doubly critical because it gave the Tripolitans their most powerful warship. Stephen Decatur volunteered for an extremely perilous mission. On the night of February 16, 1804, he and a company of volunteers glided into the heavily fortified harbor of Tripoli in a captured ketch, aptly renamed* Intrepid. *Decatur's men swarmed aboard* Philadelphia, *routed her pirate crew, and set the frigate blazing from stem to stern. They were away within twenty minutes and, as guns of shore batteries and anchored corsairs roared,* Intrepid *escaped without the loss of a man. England's most famous sea lord, Horatio Nelson, called it "the most bold and daring act of the age."*

Barbary Pirates

In 1803, Commodore Edward Preble was assigned to lead an expedition against the Barbary States. This pirate league — Morocco, Algiers, Tunis, and Tripoli — controlled most of the North African coast and had preyed upon the trade of the Christian nations of Europe for three hundred years.

The United States already had some ships in the Mediterranean when Preble arrived with *Constitution.* By November of 1803, the Commodore commanded a well-led force which included *Philadelphia,* a 36-gun frigate (commanded by William Bainbridge); *Argus,* 16 guns (Isaac Hull); *Siren,* 16 guns (Charles Stewart); *Vixen,* 14 guns (John Smith); *Nautilus,* 12 guns (Richard Somers); and *Enterprise,* 12 guns (Stephen Decatur).

Preble summoned the commanding officers to a conference in his cabin after the squadron assembled off the African coast and was disappointed to find none was even thirty years old. Preble was forty-two. Later, when chided for referring to the officers as "boys," Preble quickly amended: "Yes, but they are good boys." This was prophetic, because four — Hull, Bainbridge, Stewart, and Decatur — were among *Constitution*'s later commanders.

Preble was one of the ablest mariners of his time. He had left his home on a Maine farm at sixteen to serve at sea in the War of Independence and briefly was a prisoner of the British. After the war he saw much of the world during fifteen years in the merchant marine. He was commissioned as a Navy lieutenant in 1798 and promoted to captain the next year.

At the outset, Preble's severe insistence on proficiency made him unpopular with his command, but under him not a single court-martial was held on *Constitution,* and his ability to inspire and train his subordinates produced many of the Navy's most renowned heroes.

Few naval commanders ever operated in a more perilous area. Headquarters for the pirates were at Algiers, Tunis, and Tripoli, along some six hundred miles of the North African Mediterranean shore. This meant a northeasterly wind could trap sailing ships by stranding them along the pirate-controlled coast. If driven ashore, a ship's crew could hope for nothing better than cruel enslavement.

Here is an entry from *Constitution*'s log:

> The weather to the northward has every appearance of a strong breeze from that quarter. A heavy gale from the N.E. or the N.N.E. would make our situation very disagreeable. It would expose us to an enemy's coast, the angular position of which to the Northward and Westward makes it necessary to avoid that part by standing to the Eastward. We could only lay the coast along and of course afford no drift or leeway. The horrors of shipwreck added to irretrievable slavery makes the coast very dangerous in the winter. If any cruises on this coast in a heavy gale on shore, they have no other safety but their sails, and if they once lose them, they lose all hopes of a retreat.

To guard against being trapped, Preble's first move was to safeguard his supply route through the narrow Straits of Gibraltar. He did this by appearing in force before Morocco and exacting a lasting treaty from the Emperor. Preble's ultimatum left no room for quibbling. He notified the American consul in Tangier:

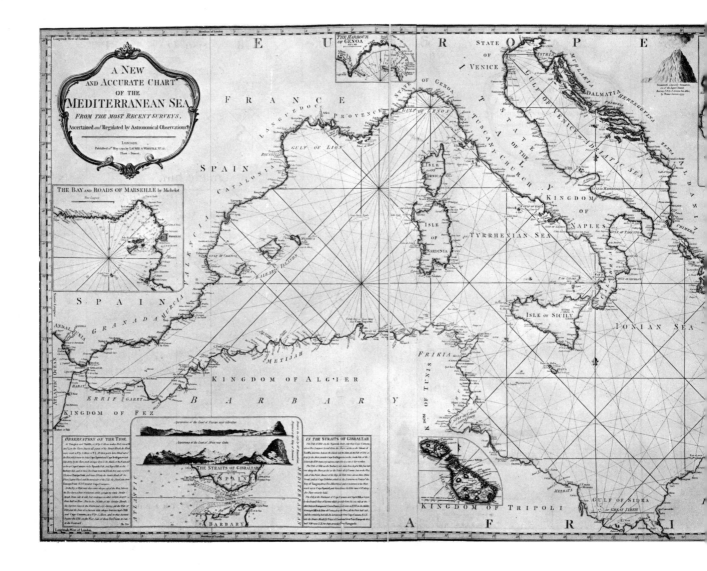

U.S.S. *Constitution,* Tangier Bay,
Six P.M. Oct. 4, 1803

I am honored with your communication of this evening. I shall not send a boat on shore until I have the Emperor's permission, but shall wait your communication by a shore boat.

As you think it will gratify his Imperial Majesty, I shall salute him and dress ship; and if he is not disposed to be pacific, *I will salute him again.*

Respectfully,
E. Preble.

Preble had no intention of waiting for a formal declaration of war by his government if the Emperor refused. His ships were ready for action; the men were sleeping beside their guns. But the quick signing of a treaty with only minor mutual concessions and no payment of tribute, secured his communications route. On November 20, Preble declared Tripoli blockaded. He was in the process of establishing a base at Syracuse, on the island of Sicily, when he learned of the loss of the frigate *Philadelphia.* This was the greatest reverse suffered in the entire campaign, because she represented approximately a third of the squadron's power. Preble had left *Philadelphia* and some other vessels patrolling Tripoli and in his absence

34

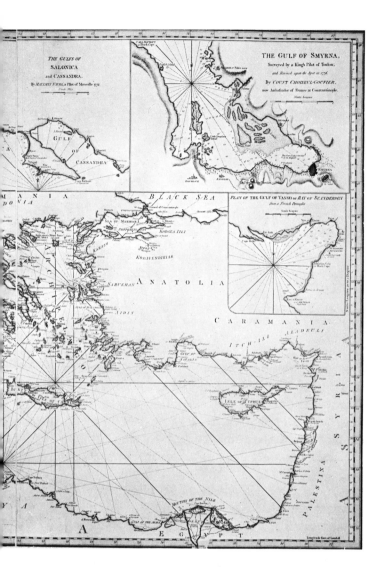

PREBLE'S SEA — *Commodore Edward Preble of* Constitution *led his squadron into the Mediterranean in 1803 to end three centuries of plundering by the piratical Barbary States. Preble's first move was to extract a treaty from the Emperor of Morocco at Tangier (1), which guaranteed him free use of the narrow Straits of Gibraltar (2). The other pirate states strung along the North African Coast were Algiers (3), Tunis (4), and Tripoli (5). Preble established his base at Syracuse (6). This chart, published in London in May of 1794, might well have been used in the operations.*

Captain Bainbridge ventured too close to the treacherous harbor; *Philadelphia* had run into uncharted rocks.

Philadelphia's guns could not be brought to bear on a fleet of attacking Tripolitan gunboats. She surrendered, and her crew of more than three hundred officers and men began many months of enslavement. A few days later, a storm brought an unusually high tide which lifted *Philadelphia* off the reef and she became, briefly, an important addition to the dey's forces. Officially, Bainbridge was held blameless for the loss, but he was severely criticized in some quarters.

BOMBARDMENT — *Preble's squadron assaulted the pirate stronghold at Tripoli on August 3, 1804. The loss of* Philadelphia *left him with only one heavily armed three-masted vessel, his flagship* Constitution. *She is shown approaching the fortifications with an assorted squadron. From left to right are* Enterprise, Nautilus, Argus, Siren, *and* Vixen, *ranging in armament from 12 to 16 guns; a mortar boat, a gunboat,* Constitution *and another gunboat at extreme right. Stephen Decatur directed the three gunboats in the center background. The fourth gunboat close to shore was commanded by his brother James, the only officer killed in the attack.*

Constitution went to her base at Syracuse, where one of the most hazardous exploits in naval history was carefully and secretly planned. A small Tripolitan trading ketch that had been captured and renamed *Intrepid* was fitted out. Stephen Decatur, one of Preble's "good boys," was given the mission of entering Tripoli Harbor and burning *Philadelphia.* Decatur had volunteered for the undertaking, intending to use his own 12-gun *Enterprise,* but it was decided *Intrepid* was less likely to attract attention. Her crew of approximately seventy-five were all volunteers. The majority were from *Enterprise,* plus five midshipmen from *Constitution* and a Maltese pilot, Salvadore Catalano, who later became a sailing master in the U. S. Navy.

After a series of delays caused by foul weather, *Intrepid* appeared before Tripoli at dusk the night of February 16, 1804, and in the dim light of a new moon crept cautiously up the harbor. Only enough men to handle the little ketch were visible, their shipmates remaining below the bulwarks.

As *Intrepid* approached, Catalano identified her as a Maltese trader that had lost her anchors in a storm, and asked permission to tie up alongside *Philadelphia.* The Moors discovered the deception too late. The Americans were already swarming aboard the frigate and corsairs leaped into the sea to escape. Each of the boarders knew his part well and within twenty minutes their firebrands had *Philadelphia* blazing from stem to stern. The flames literally drove the raiders back to *Intrepid.*

With the entire port alerted, *Intrepid*'s departure was far more hazardous than her arrival. Her crew churned the water to froth with the ketch's sixteen long oars as they ran a gauntlet of gunfire from shore batteries and surrounding Tripolitan gunboats. Not the least of the din was caused by discharge of *Philadelphia*'s loaded guns as flames touched them off.

Back at Syracuse three days later, Decatur boarded *Constitution* with his report for Commodore Preble. An entry in *Constitution*'s log recording destruction of "the late United States Frigate *Philadelphia*" concluded: "The business being so well planned not a man was killed or wounded on our side. The Tripolitans had 20 killed, the

36

others made their escape by jumping overboard after the ship was afire.''

Now came months of intense activity for *Constitution,* during which she was at sea most of the time. The squadron's manpower totaled little more than a thousand, opposing a force estimated at twenty-five thousand. *Constitution* was supported by about fifteen vessels. Tripoli Harbor was a hornets' nest of dozens of strongly armed craft, which were protected by the walled city's batteries of more than a hundred large caliber guns.

Neither the heavy odds nor his own failing health deterred Preble. Within a month, six direct assaults were made on the citadel. In the first of these, August 3, 1804, the entire American force came into point-blank range off the westerly entrances to the harbor. A score or more Tripolitan gunboats came out to meet the attack, and the Moors learned for the first time what they could expect from the U. S. Navy. *Constitution* laid down a heavy bombardment, but the fiercest fighting was hand-to-hand combat between crews of the smaller craft. A shift in the wind forced the American fleet to draw away from the dangerous lee shore, but not before it inflicted heavy damage. The town panicked. A minaret was toppled, three of the dey's gunboats were captured, and many of his men were killed or wounded.

American casualties were light by comparison and none of the ships were seriously damaged. *Constitution* suffered some injury to sails, rigging, and the foremast.

The dey sent word he would consider negotiated terms, but since no flag of truce appeared on his castle, Preble decided to attack again on the 7th. Rough weather prevented *Constitution* from drawing close enough to bring her guns to bear and the assault was executed by the smaller vessels. Again the town was heavily damaged by gunfire but the Tripolitan vessels remained well within the harbor, sheltered by rocks.

The next attack opened the night of August 24, with the small craft again initiating the action. Because of lack of wind, they had to resort to oars. Bombardment continued until dawn, but little damage was inflicted.

The assault was resumed four nights later with the smaller vessels again in the lead. They gained a position close to the rocks and bombarded every available target. They withdrew at dawn and *Constitution* moved in alone. Preble's report to the Secretary of the Navy describes the action, although it makes only slight reference to the heavy fire from shore batteries:

> We continued running in, until we were within musket shot of the Crown and Mole batteries, when we brought to, and fired upwards of three hundred round shot, besides grape and cannister, into the town, Bashaw's castle, and batteries. We silenced the castle and two of the batteries for some time. At a quarter past six, the gunboats being all out of shot and in tow, I hauled off, after having been three quarters of an hour in close action. The gunboats fired upwards of four hundred round shot, besides grape and cannister, with good effect. A large Tunisian galliot was sunk in the mole — a Spanish Seignoir received considerable damage. The Tripoline galleys and gunboats lost many men and were much cut.

Constitution also suffered battle damage, but not enough to cripple her, and Preble prepared for a fifth assault against the pirate stronghold. This was carried out September 3, with *Constitution* firing eleven broadsides into the town and shore batteries. Then the wind shifted and the squadron was compelled to withdraw.

Action against the corsairs ended the next night on a mysterious and tragic note. *Intrepid*, which served Decatur in burning *Philadelphia*, had been prepared as a fire ship, laden with a hundred barrels of powder. She was guided into the harbor by Captain Richard Somers of *Nautilus* and other volunteers. It was hoped disaster would be inflicted on the enemy's fleet, but she and her crew vanished in the blinding flash of a premature explosion. The tremendous blast did cause considerable damage, but *Intrepid* had not reached the main concentration of shipping.

The squadron was due for another disappointment. On September 10, the frigates *President* and *Constellation* arrived with

Commodore Samuel Barron to take over command. The relief of Preble was not a reflection on him, but he and his command felt it keenly. Officially, he was highly commended, but many felt he had been shabbily treated after drubbing the corsairs into submission, leaving little for successors to do but conclude treaties ending their plunders.

Preble may have been unpopular when he came aboard, but as he departed all *Constitution*'s officers were moved to sign a letter telling him of their regret.

During his command no man had been killed while aboard and only one wounded, a marine, although on occasion grapeshot was found imbedded in *Constitution*'s stout planking. Preble came home on the frigate *John Adams*. The corsairs had been well softened when Preble was relieved and his successors were not again called on to use *Constitution*'s guns to obtain acceptable agreements. Barron's arrival with four additional frigates and the capture of a corsair stronghold at Derne by a land force under Captain William Eaton greatly strengthened the American position. Preble had proven the power the Yankees could exert from the sea. The dey of Tripoli now was ready for peace.

Illness caused Commodore Barron to turn over the command of the Mediterranean squadron to Commodore John Rodgers, who lost no time in demanding a showdown from the dey. A treaty was drawn in *Constitution*'s cabin, signed in June 1805, under which $60,000 was paid for release of American captives but which called for no further tribute.

His greed whetted by Tripoli's success in extorting large sums of money, the ruler of neighboring Tunis, the bey, indicated he, too, felt entitled to raid the U. S. Treasury. Rodgers thought differently, and on August 1 anchored most of his force off Tunis. His method was very similar to that used by Preble in bringing Morocco to terms at the start

AN AVENGING BROTHER —
*James Decatur was shot through the
head by the captain of a Tripolitan
vessel which had feigned surrender.
His brother, Stephen, the hero of the
burning of* Philadelphia, *pursued,
boarded, and captured the Tripolitan
craft. It is reported that in the raging
free-for-all that followed, Stephen's
sword was broken and one of his own
men charged in and saved him from a
death blow. This is a romanticized version of the hand-to-hand battle.*

FROM THE SHORES OF TRIPOLI · 1805

of the campaign. Rodgers sent the American Consul General the following ultimatum:

> He [the bey] must do one of three things, by simple request, or else do all three by force. He must give the guarantee already required — or, he must give sufficient security for peace and send a minister to the United States — or, he must make such alterations in the treaty as you may require, and as may satisfy you that there is confidence to be placed in what he does.
>
> I have only to repeat, that if he does not do all that is necessary and proper, at the risk of my conduct being disapproved by my country, he shall feel the vengeance of the squadron now in the bay.

A treaty was promptly signed ending any demand for payment of tribute to Tunis.

Constitution remained on the Mediterranean station until 1807 to guarantee continued good behavior by the commerce raiders. Then she came home to spend two years at the New York Navy Yard. Several calmer voyages followed, including transport of some of our diplomatic agents to foreign posts.

Under command of Captain Isaac Hull, she returned to the United States and underwent considerable repair at the Washington Navy Yard, which put her in excellent condition for the War of 1812.

On one of her earlier visits to Gibraltar she had been in company with a Yankee brig, and had greatly impressed England's great sea lord, Horatio Nelson, who observed *Constitution* and those who handled her so smartly. He said, "In the handling of those trans-Atlantic ships there is a nucleus of trouble for the Navy of Great Britain."

In 1803, Napoleon had anticipated Britain's troubles with the Americans. After signing the agreement for the Louisiana Purchase he said, "I have this day given Britain a maritime rival who will sooner or later humble her pride."

One of the country's most important gains in the Barbary campaign was that it provided the Navy with a seasoned corps of highly proficient young officers. Many of those who won fame during the War of 1812 had their training in Preble's off-shore school. These officers were proud to be known as "Preble's 'boys.'"

"TO THE SHORES OF TRIPOLI" — *Capture of the grim fortification at Derne inspired the line in the Marine Corps anthem. It was taken April 26, 1805, by an overland expedition led by Captain William Eaton, which marched six hundred miles across the desert from Alexandria. The force included a detail of marines under Lieutenant Presley O'Bannon and had support from the guns of three ships of Preble's old squadron. Eaton was severely wounded in the assault and O'Bannon took command. The Tripolitan banner was hauled down and for the first time in the country's history the flag of the United States was raised over a fortress of the Old World.*

"WHITE ASH BREEZE" —

Constitution *had scarcely begun her first cruise in the War of 1812 when she was almost trapped by a five-ship British squadron. The wind was so light that all the ships lost steerageway when* Constitution *was just beyond the range of enemy guns. Skill, resourcefulness, and back-breaking toil by Captain Isaac Hull and his crew saved her. First an attempt was made to keep* Constitution *out of harm's way by resorting to a "white ash breeze" — oars — and towing her with the ship's boats. Then an anchor was carried out ahead, dropped, and* Constitution *was hauled up to it. The British promptly adopted the Yankee tactics and in a three-day slow-motion chase* Constitution's *crew had little food or rest. She finally made good her escape when Hull outfoxed the British in a rain squall: as the storm approached* Constitution, *Hull had her sails hastily taken in; the alarmed British followed suit. But Hull's seeming caution was a trick. As soon as* Constitution *was hidden by the rain he immediately reset all her sails. She was away at an eleven-knot clip.*

Escape

There was little reason for optimism when Congress declared war on Britain on June 18, 1812. The new Navy had only a score of warships. The Royal Navy had six to seven hundred armed vessels, including numerous line-of-battle ships. The United States had no ships of this size and could not afford combat with the enemy's more powerful warships. Many of England's ships were engaged in fighting a bitter war with France, but this did not cancel a great difference between the two navies.

Although *Constitution* is best known for victories, one of her escapes must be considered almost as important as any single battle. Only a month after the declaration of war, she escaped from a squadron of five British warships which together mounted well over two hundred guns against the fifty-five *Constitution* probably carried at the time. Skill, daring, and the most demanding labor made possible her continued life and later victories.

Constitution was bound up the coast from Chesapeake Bay for New York, where Captain Isaac Hull expected to join the squadron of Commodore John Rodgers. Instead, there was a very confused meeting with the British ships off the New Jersey shore on July 17. Hull at first mistook them for Rodgers's squadron, and the British commanders also had difficulty separating friend from foe. The British vessels, under Commodore P. V. B. Broke, were the 64-gun ship *Africa*, 38-gun frigates *Shannon* and *Bel-*

videra, 32-gun frigate *Aeolus*, and the 38-gun frigate *Guerriere*, last to join the rendezvous.

The light breeze dropped to a flat calm at nightfall and left the six ships scattered and drifting aimlessly on a glassy sea. Dawn, however, brought recognition, and a chase immediately started with *Constitution* as the lone quarry. Shots were exchanged but caused little damage. The wind continued too light to furnish steerageway and finally the belligerents resorted to the oars of their ships' boats which were pressed into service to propel the warships. But with the enemy gaining, Hull prepared to make a stand and go down fighting. He later gave his first lieutenant, Charles Morris, full credit for a suggestion which probably saved *Constitution* — use of a kedge anchor. A member of the crew described the operation. In his pamphlet, "Naval Scenes In the Last War," one of *Constitution*'s crew members, gunner Moses Smith, reported:

Captain Hull came aft, cooly surveyed the scene, took a match in his hand, and ordered the quarter-master to hoist the American flag. I stood within a few feet of Hull at the time. He clapped the fire to my gun, No. 1, and such a barking as sounded over the sea! It was worth hearing. No sooner had our iron dog opened his mouth in this manner, than the whole enemy opened the whole of theirs. Every one of the ships fired directly toward us. Those nearest kept up their firing for some time; but of course not a shot reached us then, at the distance we were.

Captain Hull gave up the match to the captain of the gun, and we kept blazing away with our stern chasers. The shots we fired helped send us ahead, out of the reach of the enemy. There was little or no wind; but we resolved to save ourselves from capture, or sink in the conflict. We soon found, however, that we made but slow work in getting ahead.

Hull called Lieutenant Morris to him and said calmly, "Let's lay broadside to them, Mr. Morris, and fight the whole! If they sink us, we'll go down like men!"

We were off Little Egg Harbour, on the New Jersey shore, at the time stretching in toward the Delaware Bay. The enemy had drawn in between us and the land so that the prospect was they might cut us off from the Capes.

Mr. Morris now spoke to Captain Hull: "There is one thing, sir, I think we'd better try."

"What's that?" replied Hull.

"Try to kedge her off" [a method for moving a ship by carrying out an anchor and then drawing the vessel up to it] said the lieutenant.

All available cordage was joined to the anchor cable and two ship's boats carried the hook out ahead and dropped it. *Constitution* then was hauled to the anchor with the capstan. This back-breaking task was repeated throughout the night, with all hands working. Although the British promptly imitated the procedure, *Constitution* still was out of range at dawn, and when a breeze sprang up *Constitution* left her pursuers to leeward and ended three days of peril.

The escape astonished the British commanders, who scarcely could have been more chagrined if they had lost one of their own ships.

Not wishing to risk meeting blockading forces off New York, Hull shaped a course for Boston, arriving after twenty-two days at sea. There he issued a statement requesting that plaudits directed to him be distributed among his "brave officers and crew." The statement concluded: "Captain Hull has great pleasure in saying, that notwithstanding the length of the chase, and the officers and crew being deprived of sleep, and allowed but little refreshment during the time, not a murmur was heard to escape them."

Guerriere

If Captain Isaac Hull had waited for orders, *Constitution* might never have scored her most celebrated victory over the British frigate *Guerriere.*

When *Constitution* returned to Boston after the fox-and-hounds chase with Broke's squadron, Hull's orders had not arrived. Hull knew he was risking his naval career, but he felt it wiser to get to sea than be trapped by a British blockade. Ironically, when the orders did reach Boston they read to remain in port.

Constitution sailed from Boston August 2, 1812, and on the 19th found *Guerriere* some six hundred miles to the eastward. The ships sighted each other about two in the afternoon, but Hull had no notion of following the British doctrine of naval warfare laid down by Lord Nelson — "Never mind manoeuvres, always go at them." Instead, he made careful preparations and kept a favorable windward position until he was satisfied it was time to close with the enemy. *Guerriere,* which the British had captured from the French in 1806, was under the command of Captain James Dacres.

Moses Smith, describing the meeting with *Guerriere,* wrote:

Before all hands could be called, there was a general rush on deck. The word passed like lightning from man to man; and all who could be spared, came flocking up like pigeons from a net bed. From the spar deck to the gun deck, from that to the berth deck, every man was roused and on his feet. All eyes were turned in the direction of the strange sail, and quick as thought, studding-sails were out, fore and aft. The noble frigate fairly bounded over the billows, as we gave her a rap full, and spread her broad and tall wings to the gale.

The stranger hauled his wind, and laid to for us. It was evident that he was an English man-of-war of a large class and all ready for action. . . .

As we came up she began to fire. They were evidently trying to rake us. But we continued on our course, tacking and half-tacking, taking good care to avoid being raked. We came so near on one tack, that an eighteen-pound shot came through us under the larboard [port] knight-head, striking just abaft the breech of the gun to which I belonged. The splinters flew in all directions; but no one was hurt. We immediately picked up the shot, and put it in the mouth of long Tom, a large gun loose on deck — and sent it home again, with our respects.

Another stray shot hit our foremast, cutting one of the hoops in two. But the mast was not otherwise injured, and the slight damage was soon repaired.

Hull was now all animation. He saw that the decisive moment had come. With great energy, yet calmness of manner, he passed around among the officers and men, addressing to them words of confidence and encouragement.

"Men," said he, "now do your duty. Your officers cannot have entire command over you now. Each man must do all in his power for his country."

DRAMA ON THE HIGH SEAS —
Only one month after Constitution *eluded the British squadron, she found* Guerriere, *one of her recent pursuers, some six hundred miles east of Boston. The series of paintings by Thomas Birch (above and on the following two pages) graphically depicts phases of the meeting. Here,* Constitution's *men are aloft and on the bowsprit shortening sail in preparation for the impending battle. The originals of this series are the property of the United States Naval Academy. President John Fitzgerald Kennedy borrowed them to hang in his White House office.*

47

As Hull maneuvered to bring the guns to bear, he told the impatient crew; "You shall have her as close as you please. Sailing master! lay her alongside!"

A devastating broadside from guns doubleshotted with round and grape swept *Guerriere*. The two ships engaged in a furious exchange, with the British firing more rapidly but with little accuracy. Much of *Guerriere*'s fire went into *Constitution*'s rigging. *Constitution* concentrated on her foe's hull. *Guerriere*'s mizzenmast was shot away within fifteen minutes of Hull's first broadside.

After surging ahead of *Guerriere*, Hull brought *Constitution* about, intending to cross her bow to rake the enemy ship, but because of damage to her rigging, *Constitution* was difficult to manage. As a result, *Guerriere* drove her bowsprit and jib boom into *Constitution*'s mizzen rigging. As the ships drew apart, *Guerriere*'s fore- and mainmasts also came crashing down, leaving her a helpless, wallowing wreck. Efforts of her

OLD IRONSIDES — *Above,* Constitution *ranges alongside and, keeping her fire low, inflicts devastating injury to* Guerriere*'s hull. The foe's mizzenmast was shot away almost at the outset of the battle.*

Above right, the antagonists crash together in heavy seas with Guerriere*'s bowsprit flailing* Constitution*'s quarterdeck. As the two ships draw apart,* Guerriere*'s shattered fore- and mainmasts also go by the board.*

Below right, Guerriere *is a dismasted, helpless hulk after* Constitution*'s most celebrated victory, from which she emerged without critical damage. A Yankee gunner who saw a shot bounce off* Constitution*'s oaken planking shouted: "Her sides are made of iron!" Thus she earned the name by which she is best known to millions — Old Ironsides.*

48

crew to get her under control were futile, and after *Constitution* made emergency repairs and again approached her. *Guerriere* fired a gun to leeward in token of surrender.

At the height of this engagement *Constitution* earned the nickname by which she became best known to generations of Americans — Old Ironsides. According to legend, a gunner aboard *Constitution* saw a British shot bounce off her oaken planking and exclaimed; "Her sides are made of iron!"

Deeds of daring were commonplace. The Navy commemorated one in 1919 by naming a destroyer in memory of an Irish lad named Daniel Hogan, who served during this battle as an ordinary seaman: "During the engagement with the British frigate *Guerriere,* when the flag was shot away from the foretop-gallant masthead, he climbed up and lashed it in place in the face of the firing."

When the battle was over, a boarding party from *Constitution* saw that *Guerriere* was too badly damaged to be brought home as a prize, so the 267 survivors were taken aboard *Constitution*. At Hull's orders *Guer-*

riere was set afire and she disappeared in a tremendous explosion when flames reached her magazines.

Constitution had proved herself superior to her foe in every respect. While records were not kept with any uniformity it is surmised that she carried fifty-five guns and could deliver a broadside of 684 pounds. *Guerriere* is believed to have carried forty-nine guns, with a broadside potential of 556 pounds. *Constitution* is believed to have carried a crew of 456, of whom seven were killed, one accidentally by the misfire of one of her own guns. Her displacement was given at 1,576 tons. *Guerriere*'s crew was listed at 282, fifteen of whom were killed, and her displacement at 1,338 tons.

Constitution returned to Boston with her prisoners on August 30, 1812, and was given an exuberant welcome. The victory gave a much-needed lift to the country, whose battles ashore were not going well.

The return also brought a change in command. Hull, after two years, turned the command of Old Ironsides over to his friend Commodore William Bainbridge.

50

A HARD-WON WAGER — *In a cordial meeting before the war, the captains Hull and Dacres had wagered a hat on the outcome if* Constitution *ever met* Guerriere *in combat. It is reported that they engaged in the following exchange when Dacres came aboard as a prisoner from the helpless wreck of* Guerriere, *left.*

"Dacres, my dear fellow, I am glad to see you on board," said Hull, advancing and offering his hand.

"D--n it, Hull," responded Dacres, "I suppose you are"; and, unbuckling his sword, he offered it to his captor.

"I will not take a sword from one who knows so well how to use it," said Captain Hull; "but, I tell you, Dacres, I will trouble you for that hat."

THE SPIRIT OF 1812 — Constitution*'s men had the best of reasons for enthusiasm. They fought not only for ship and country but for freedom on the high seas. This old print shows a gun crew at its station during the battle with* Guerriere, *jubilant over the striking of a telling blow. But the young boy who carried the explosives, the powder monkey, is not diverted as he speeds to feed the loud-mouthed iron dog. This defeat of a British ship had great significance for both sides: it did much to dispel the illusion that the British Navy was invincible, and it brought confidence to both the young American Navy and the nation.*

Java

Constitution's crew was so openly dissatisfied when Commodore William Bainbridge succeeded Isaac Hull as commanding officer that some of the more outspoken were ordered off the ship to other duty. Disappointment over losing Hull had something to do with the crew's discontent. Furthermore, Bainbridge was known as a stern disciplinarian with his men.

Old Ironsides left Boston on October 27, 1812, for the West Indies, and a record of numerous punishments indicates that she was not a happy ship. Her triumph over the British frigate *Java* improved morale.

Constitution encountered *Java* off the Brazilian coast the morning of December 29. The battle which followed paralleled, in some respects, Hull's victory over *Guerriere*. *Java*'s firepower was slightly greater than *Guerriere*'s. She was faster and carried many more men, probably over four hundred, since she had a considerable number aboard en route to duty elsewhere. *Java* had been captured from the French and, like *Guerriere*, was considered better than most British frigates of the same class.

Constitution drew *Java* away from the coast to gain sea room in which to fight. It was well into the afternoon before Bainbridge felt he was a sufficient distance from shore. He turned, headed straight for *Java*, and fired an opening broadside from almost the maximum range of *Constitution*'s long 24-pounders. The Commodore's strategy was to weaken *Java* as much as possible with long guns before coming within range of the foe's carronades. *Java* repeatedly tried to cross *Constitution*'s bow to rake her and as many times was treated to a broadside from Old Ironsides before she tacked away in a screen of powder smoke. *Java* was unsuccessful, too, in attempts to board her enemy.

Within an hour, all *Java*'s spars were shot away. Commodore Bainbridge's journal furnishes this account:

> At forty minutes past two, determined to close with the enemy notwithstanding his raking. Set the fore-and mainsail and luffed up close to him. At fifty minutes past two the enemy's jib-boom got foul of our mizzen rigging. At three the head of the enemy's bowsprit and jib-boom were shot away by us. At five minutes past three, shot away the enemy's foremast by the board. At fifteen minutes past three, shot away his main top mast just above the cap. At forty minutes past three, shot away the gaff and spanker boom. At fifty-five minutes past three, shot away his mizzenmast nearly by the board.

Of *Java*'s spars, only a stub of the mainmast remained, and fallen wreckage made it impossible to man most of her guns. *Constitution* drew away and made temporary repairs while, aboard *Java,* a futile attempt was being made to restore her to fighting trim. But her condition was hopeless and, when *Constitution* approached, *Java* struck her colors. About fifty of her crew were dead or dying and about a hundred had been wounded. Her commander, Captain Henry Lambert, died soon after reaching shore.

Constitution had lost twelve men and twenty-two were wounded, including Bainbridge.

Examination showed that, as with *Guerriere*, there was no hope of bringing *Java* home as a prize. After survivors were taken off, she was set afire; like *Guerriere,* the explosion of her magazines sank her. The prisoners were landed at Sao Salvador (Bahai), on the coast of Brazil, and Old Ironsides returned to Boston, her home port, the last day of February 1813 to another victory celebration. *Constitution* went to the Boston Navy Yard for a needed overhaul.

Before relinquishing command to become commander of the Yard, Bainbridge performed a service that must have done much to win favor with the crew. Prize money had been voted by Congress for the destruction of *Guerriere* but never received, and an additional award of $50,000 was made for destroying *Java.* Bainbridge prodded the government, and both awards were promptly paid.

The victories caused consternation in England while stirring the United States Congress to authorize, belatedly, four new line-of-battle ships and six frigates. The war ended before they got to sea, and our dwindling fleet saw it to a close.

It was said in some quarters that the American frigates were ships-of-the-line in disguise and that this gave them an unfair military advantage. Britishers who protested that introduction of the new frigates was not altogether sporting — not quite cricket, perhaps — failed to consider other factors. The American victories also represented superior gunnery, sail-handling, and strategy by eager sailormen who had volunteered their services to their country. Previous hostile acts by the Barbary pirates, France, and England had idled numerous American merchant ships, making many experienced seamen available for naval duty. Before the war ended, England attempted to build new frigates and cut down line-of-battle ships in the hope of meeting our frigates on more equal terms.

Naval victories counteracted the discouragement caused by numerous reverses in the war ashore.

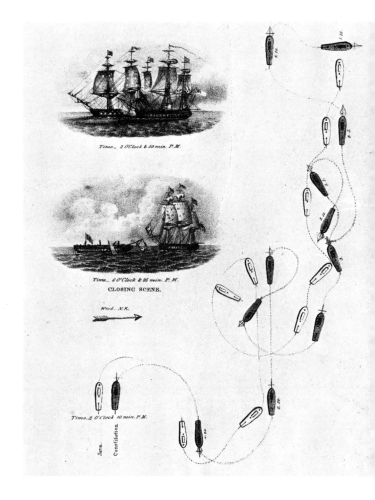

FIERCEST FRIGATE ACTION OF THE WAR — Constitution *reduced* Java *to a lumbering hulk through the same deliberate method used to dispose of* Guerriere. *The illustrations, particularly those inserted in the sailing diagram, clearly show damage to* Constitution *sails; British gunners kept their fire high, while the Yankees probed for the heart of their quarry in the hull itself.* Constitution *emerged damaged but not out of control, while* Java *was so badly injured she could not be brought home as a prize. Before the battle ended,* Constitution *had shot away all of* Java's *spars. The defeat of* Java *caused the British Admiralty to issue orders that their frigates were not to engage the 44-gun American frigates in any single action.*

U.S.S. *CONSTITUTION* DEFEATS H.M.S. *JAVA*
December 29, 1812

Cyane — Levant

Under Captain Charles Stewart, who had succeeded Commodore Bainbridge, *Constitution* left Boston on the last day of 1813 to raid British commerce. In three months at sea, she took only a few merchant prizes, and destroyed the 14-gun *Pictou* before heading home.

Old Ironsides' career almost ended within sight of her home port of Boston at the conclusion of this cruise.

It had been Stewart's intention to put in at Portsmouth, New Hampshire, but a shift in wind made this impossible and a course was set for Boston. On April 3, 1814, *Constitution* worked down the coast in a light breeze which fell to a flat calm just as two 38-gun British frigates, *Tenedos* and *Junon,* bore down on her, taking advantage of a brisk breeze that had not reached *Constitution*. Having passed Cape Ann and Gloucester Harbor, she was pinned against Massachusetts's rocky North Shore with escape by sea cut off. Stewart wanted to seek refuge in Salem Harbor, but no one aboard was familiar with its difficult approaches. Marblehead was the only alternative, and Stewart had to take this long chance. As the British ships continued to gain, all goods aboard that could be spared were jettisoned to lighten the ship and increase her speed. Over the side went spare spars, stores, and valuable prize merchandise. The fresh water and the spirits were pumped overboard. These sacrifices paid off, for soon *Constitution* gained the security of the little harbor. There she was protected by the guns of Fort Sewall and the militia which rallied from coastal towns. The British decided not to test the defense and sailed away. A few days later *Constitution* came down to Boston where she was blockaded eight and a half months.

She received jubilant receptions on her earlier victorious returns to her home port, but it soon became apparent some of the cheering had been by fair weather friends. Pressure was brought to have *Constitution* leave the Navy Yard and move down the harbor, where the blockading fleet could get at her without damaging the town, but this proposal that Old Ironsides become a sacrificial offering was successfully resisted. Finally, on December 18, 1814, while winter weather disrupted the blockade, Stewart slipped *Constitution* out of the harbor and clear of the land.

This was *Constitution*'s last war cruise.

She took two British merchantmen, but the voyage was otherwise uneventful until February 20, 1815, when the 34-gun frigate *Cyane* and the 20-gun sloop *Levant* were sighted and pursued off the Madeira Islands.

The meeting was late in the afternoon. Maneuvers of the British commanders, Captain Gordon Falcon of *Cyane* and Captain the Honorable George Douglass of *Levant,* indicated they wished to delay action in hope of a better opportunity to disable *Constitution* in darkness.

Stewart had other plans, and the engagement opened as the sun set. Broadsides were exchanged with *Cyane,* about three hundred yards to leeward, and hot action developed. The moon appeared but visibility was reduced by mist and gunsmoke. *Constitution* drew abeam of *Levant* and belted her with a broadside as *Cyane* came up astern intending to rake *Constitution*. Then Stewart executed a difficult piece of sail-handling: he backed *Constitution* down, poured heavy fire into *Cyane,* and hit *Levant* with two additional broadsides. *Levant* was forced to drop out of the fray temporarily. *Cyane* tried to run off

before the wind, but *Constitution* raked her over the stern. Hopelessly crippled, *Cyane* surrendered, forty minutes after the engagement opened. *Levant* tried to get back into the engagement alone, but she was quickly overpowered by Old Ironsides.

Stewart's skill in handling *Constitution* had enabled her to wear down *Cyane* and *Levant* without having had to take their combined fire simultaneously. *Cyane* and *Levant* had a total of 763 pounds of metal in their combined broadsides, compared with *Constitution*'s 704.

Of *Constitution*'s crew of 451, six were killed and nine wounded. Between *Cyane* and *Levant,* with crews totaling 320, nineteen were killed and forty-two wounded.

THE CURTAIN COMES DOWN

— Constitution *fought her last battle under the command of Captain Charles Stewart near the Madeira Islands off the African coast. There she encountered the British frigate* Cyane *and the sloop-of-war* Levant *on February 20, 1815.* Constitution *whittled down the strength of each separately.* Cyane *was subdued first.* Levant *withdrew from the action long enough to repair her rigging and returned to the fray, but* Cyane *had already struck her colors; after a quick exchange of gunfire,* Levant *was persuaded to surrender.*

AFTER THE BATTLE — Constitution *takes battered* Cyane *in tow for haven in a neutral port. Although the island port reached was neutral, Stewart did not feel secure there and, on March 10, 1815, when several large ships approached through the fog, he ordered the anchor cables cut.* Constitution *and the two prizes fled to sea. An unsuccessful chase by three frigates of Captain Sir George Collier's squadron was described in the* Naval History of Great Britain, *published in London in 1837, as "the most blundering piece of business recorded in these six volumes."*

Cyane suffered thirty-eight casualties from her complement of 180. Levant's casualties were twenty-three of 140.

After putting the three ships in order, Constitution sailed with Cyane and Levant for the Cape Verde Islands off the African coast to land prisoners. On March 10, while at Port Praya, her career almost ended: the sails of a large ship suddenly appeared over low-lying fog outside, then the sails of two other ships. Stewart ordered Constitution's anchor cable cut and directed his prize crews to get Cyane and Levant underway immediately. The three vessels cleared the harbor and a baffling chase began. All that was visible to the crews were the upper sails of the mystery ships above the fog. Stewart's suspicions

58

about the strangers were confirmed by English prisoners still aboard. They identified them as units of Captain Sir George Collier's squadron — the 50-gun frigates *Leander* and *Newcastle* and the 40-gun *Acasta*. *Leander* and *Newcastle* had been designed and built to excel the new class of American frigates. Collier's force had been seeking *Constitution* ever since she had eluded his blockade at Boston.

As the chase grew hot, there was some gunfire that fell short of *Constitution*. Old Ironsides' superior speed stood her in good stead, and she pursued an uneventful voyage home, by way of the West Indies, arriving in New York on May 15, 1815. *Cyane*, making a direct crossing, preceded her and had been added to our forces. *Levant* had been chased back to Port Praya, a neutral port, where she was attacked by *Newcastle* and *Acasta* although she signaled surrender. British embarrassment over permitting *Constitution* to escape was not lessened by discovery that *Levant* was not another American frigate but one of their own small vessels previously taken as a prize. Stewart's log noted: "It became necessary to separate from the *Levant* or to risk being brought into action to cover her.... The whole of the enemy's squadron tacked in pursuit of the *Levant* and gave over the pursuit of this ship.... This sacrifice of the *Levant* became necessary for the preservation of the *Constitution*."

It is worth noting that had effective communications systems been in operation, *Constitution*'s last battle would not have been fought. In the *Cyane-Levant* engagement on February 20, 1815, both sides were aware peace was near if not actually agreed upon. But in the absence of reliable information from home offices, the opposing commanders were called upon to make their own decisions and they chose, without apparent reluctance, to fight. In fact, a peace treaty already had been signed at Ghent on December 24, 1814, and ratified by the

United States on February 17, 1815. The terms allowed thirty days for word to reach distant commands and end hostilities, which legalized Old Ironsides' victory. Andrew Jackson's triumph over Major General Sir Edward Pakenham at New Orleans was scored under similar circumstances on January 8, 1815.

So ended the War of 1812. The hard-fought naval engagements closed not in bitterness but in mutual respect between the opposing forces. During the war, proposals were made for meetings of evenly matched ships, but the United States could not afford to make war a sporting event. Such balanced contests were too likely to bring equal losses and expend American's ships before the enemy's.

When earlier in the war, *Guerriere* surrendered and her wounded commander came aboard *Constitution* as a prisoner, Isaac Hull helped him over the side and declined Captain Dacres's proffered sword. In reporting, Dacres told his superiors, "I feel it my duty to state that conduct of Captain Hull and his officers to our men has been that of a brave enemy; the greatest care being taken to prevent our men losing the smallest trifle and the greatest attention being paid to the wounded."

The surrender of *Java*'s commander, Captain Lambert, was more tragic. He died of his wounds shortly after being taken ashore in Brazil. As Lambert was leaving *Constitution,* Commodore Bainbridge, severely wounded himself, was assisted on deck for a parting courtesy and to return Lambert's sword.

Lieutenant Henry Chads, who succeeded to command when Lambert was wounded, reported to the British Admiralty "grateful acknowledgement for the generous treatment Captain Lambert and his officers have experienced from our gallant enemy." Later he was quoted as saying *Constitution* was handled so skillfully "it made me regret that she was not British."

Quiet Years

Constitution came home from the wars in 1815 too sea-worn and battered to participate in a bit of unfinished business with the Algerian corsairs. While our ships were occupied with the War of 1812, the Algerians seized the opportunity to again attack our merchant ships. Two squadrons were sent to the Mediterranean, one under Commodore Stephen Decatur and the other under Commodore William Bainbridge, and the remaining Barbary pirates were subdued.

Old Ironsides remained idle six years, during which she underwent extensive repairs. Then, on May 13, 1821, she departed from Boston under the command of Captain Jacob Jones to resume duty as flagship of the Mediterranean squadron. During this cruise, *Constitution* was visited by the English poet Lord Byron.

Constitution came home to Boston in 1823 to take aboard a new crew, and after refitting, returned to the Mediterranean. This four-year tour of duty consisted largely of "showing the flag" as protection for American shipping.

Upon returning to Boston, *Constitution* was withdrawn from service on July 19, 1828. After a survey, she was pronounced unseaworthy in 1830. Her planking and decking had decayed badly, although most of her timbers were sound. The Navy Department ruled she should be sold or scrapped, a decision which so outraged a young law student, Oliver Wendell Holmes, that he composed his stirring poem "Old Ironsides."

Published in newspapers throughout the country, it rolled up such a tidal wave of protest that *Constitution*'s death warrant was quickly withdrawn. Funds were appropriated for restoration of the old frigate. At the Boston Navy Yard, on June 24, 1833, she became the first occupant of a new drydock that bears her name to this day. The operation revealed that her keel was "hogged," that is, her bow and stern had drooped — as much as two and a half feet. This distortion was variously attributed to difficulties experienced in her initial launching and the great burden of armament she had carried fore and aft. It was corrected in restoring her to a seaworthy state. What effect it may have had on her remarkable sailing qualities could not be determined. During the repairs, *Constitution* was again under command of Isaac Hull.

Reconstruction no sooner was completed in 1834 than a furious storm erupted over the installation of a new figurehead representing President Andrew Jackson.

Her original figurehead represented Her-

cules, a symbol of strength, but it was destroyed during the Barbary wars in a collision with a sister ship. It was replaced by a purely decorative billet, or fiddlehead, so called because the tops of the timbers were carved much like the scrolls on the head of a violin. Some historians claim a figure of Neptune graced *Constitution*'s prow during this period.

Jesse D. Elliott was commandant of the Boston Navy Yard in 1833, and he decided Old Ironsides deserved something more elaborate than a billet head. He could not have anticipated the fury of objections to his choice of President Jackson as the subject of a new figurehead. Jackson had many strong political opponents in Boston at that time. Elliott was threatened with bodily harm, but, with the Navy Department's approval, he arranged to have a skilled woodcarver, Laban S. Beecher, proceed with the work. Pressure — even attempted bribery — was brought to bear on Beecher to have him quit the task or dispose of the unfinished work as the project became more and more a violent political issue. To safeguard the carving, Elliott had it removed to the Navy Yard where, with an armed guard standing by, Beecher completed it.

A FIGUREHEAD OF CONTROVERSY — *A political storm broke over* Constitution *in 1834. President Andrew Jackson's political enemies violently protested the installation of a life-sized image of "Old Hickory" as Old Ironsides' figurehead. One stormy night, a Cape Cod merchant skipper, undetected by armed sentinels, sawed off the head of the image. Jackson's friends were outraged; his foes, delighted. Eventually the figurehead was repaired. An image of President Jackson decorated Old Ironsides' prow for many years. As shown at left, the figurehead is believed to have represented Jackson in his riding habit. Above is a political cartoon published by the anti-Jackson press.*

61

Some of the arguments against honoring President Jackson seem to have been reasonable. It was, at least, unusual to confer such an honor on a living person. Also, it was noted that while the president was one of the nation's most conspicuous military heroes, he had no naval experience and there were many naval heroes eligible for such an honor.

The dispute raged on but Old Hickory's image was installed beneath Old Ironsides' bowsprit in the spring of 1834. As added protection for the figurehead, *Constitution* was given a berth between two line-of-battle ships and armed marines were stationed on all three ships' bows, night and day. Despite these precautions, a merchant ship skipper from Cape Cod, on the night of July 2, 1834, rowed across the harbor to the Navy Yard at the height of a violent thunderstorm. Undetected, Samuel W. Dewey gained a position beneath the bowsprit and, sawing furiously as thunder rolled, he severed the head and returned with it to the city.

Dewey was an adventurous mariner and it is not clear if his motive was political or prankish, but he found himself regarded as a hero by Jackson's opponents in Boston and other eastern cities. The head was secretly displayed at many political meetings. An offer of a $1,000 reward by Captain Elliott and a threat to court-martial all hands at the Navy Yard failed to recover the head. It remained officially missing until Dewey himself appeared at the office of the Secretary of the Navy some six months later to voluntarily surrender the head and tell the story. When the story reached President Jackson, he was highly amused and was reported to have said, "I never did like that image! Give the man a postmaster's job!"

Elliott covered the mutilated figurehead with canvas and waited to have the controversial figurehead repaired until he sailed to New York as *Constitution*'s commander in March 1836. A likeness of Old Hickory adorned the frigate's bow some forty years

before it was replaced with another billet head.

Constitution sailed on March 16 to bring home our minister to France. The ship returned June 22, and Captain Elliott sailed again in August as commander-in-chief of the Mediterranean Squadron on a three-year tour of duty. On a call at the British Naval Station on the island of Malta in 1836 it was apparent old animosities between the United States and Great Britain were forgotten. The former enemy joined the American force in an observance of Washington's Birthday by dressing ship and the firing of national salutes by fourteen anchored ships.

Old Ironsides returned early in August 1838 and, upon arrival at Norfolk, Captain Elliott found trouble waiting. Many of the crew were dissatisfied and demanded their discharges, which were overdue. Captain Elliott was accused of treating his crew harshly. One charge, perhaps unique in naval annals, was that he quartered jackasses on the berth deck. He was bringing the long-eared passengers back to improve the breed in the United States. Elliott was court-martialed, convicted, and suspended from the Navy for four years.

In the spring of 1839, *Constitution* left for the South Pacific Station to spend two years cruising the west coast of South America. On her return to Norfolk she reported a very rough passage around Cape Horn.

She sailed again in the spring of 1844 on a voyage to China which eventually took her around the world during a four-year period. In 495 days at sea, Old Ironsides logged well over fifty thousand miles.

Her commander was Captain John Percival, known in the Navy as "Mad Jack" because of his volatile nature. Percival was said to have been impressed at seventeen from an American merchantman by the British and to have demonstrated such proficiency as a seaman that he served as foretop captain of Nelson's flagship *Victory* in the battle of Trafalgar. Whatever the truth of

RETURN TO THE SEA — *One of the Navy's earliest photographs, above, shows* Constitution *at the Portsmouth Navy Yard in 1858, being prepared for launching after an extensive restoration. The costumes of the two women visitors and the use of oxen as draft animals help confirm the date of this early photograph. Right, the figure of Andrew Jackson that graces her bow succeeded the original Jackson figurehead.*

SERVICE AS A TRAINING SHIP
— Constitution *was assigned to the Naval Academy at Annapolis in 1860 as a training ship. Instruction aboard the Navy's most famous warship must have been an inspiration to a new generation of midshipmen, already schooled in traditions established by a long roster of men who had served her well. A class of middies, below, receives gunnery instruction on the spar deck. If the artist's portrayal is accurate, midshipmen of that era must have been much younger than those of later years. However, it had been the practice of all navies to include many teenaged boys in their warship crews during the days of sail.*

CIVIL WAR DAYS — *The outbreak of the Civil War stirred apprehension over the safety of the venerable frigate. In 1861 she was spirited away from Annapolis to Newport, Rhode Island. The Naval Academy was also transferred to Newport, where Old Ironsides served as a training ship until 1865. Constitution was anchored off Fort Adams, right, then a formidable fortification at the entrance to Newport Harbor.*

this story, Percival competently guided *Constitution* on her longest voyage.

Much of her crew was ill when she called at Singapore in February of 1845, but a former enemy proved a good friend. Commodore Henry D. Chads of a British squadron came aboard to furnish assistance. As a lieutenant, thirty-two years earlier, Chads had come aboard as a prisoner after *Constitution* destroyed *Java*.

During the return voyage from the Pacific Station *Constitution* spent fifty-seven days between Manila and Honolulu, ninety-seven days between Mazatlan, on Mexico's Pacific Coast, around Cape Horn to Rio de Janeiro, and sixty-one days from that Brazilian port to Boston.

After two years in the Navy Yard, she sailed again in December of 1848 under Captain John Gwynn for the Mediterranean. It was on this cruise that a pope visited *Constitution*. The Reverend Charles W. Lyons, S.J., president of Georgetown University, gave this account:

In December 1848, the *Constitution* set out on a cruise that took her to the Mediterranean, where she cruised mostly along the Italian coast. At that time the Pope had left Rome because of troubled times, and was receiving shelter at the hands of the King of Naples.

Captain Gwynn extended an invitation to the King of Naples and Pope Pius IX to visit the *Constitution,* then lying in the Bay of Naples. The invitation was accepted, and these dignitaries were rowed to her in a boat manned by the captains of the other warships in the harbour, of which there were many. . . .

This is the first known instance of a sovereign pontiff being on American territory — for such was the deck of Old Ironsides.

While transporting our consul general D. S. McCauley to Alexandria from Tripoli, a son was born aboard to Mrs. McCauley. He was named Constitution Stewart McCauley to honor the ship and a former commander.

The cruise ended at New York, where *Constitution* again went out of commission for two years. Recommissioned December 22, 1852, she returned to her familiar Mediterranean station but was diverted to patrolling the West African coast in an effort to

MARION.   TALLAPOOSA.   CONSTITUTION. KEARSAGE. SARATOGA. POWHATAN.   PORTSMOUTH.   MINNESOTA.

U.S. NAVAL REVIEW AT HAMPTON-ROADS VA.

THE PASSING OF SAIL — Constitution *is almost obscured by smoke
from more modern warships. The
stacks on the others indicate that they
were propelled by steam as well as by
sail. The displacement of sail by steam
was stoutly opposed by many windjammer sailormen, who much pre-
ferred handling great expanses of
white canvas to shoveling coal. These
ships were gathered for a naval review
held at Hampton-Roads, Virginia
about 1877.*

end the slave trade. She was credited with
capturing at least one slave ship. She went
out of commission in 1855 at Portsmouth,
New Hampshire, where she was extensively
rebuilt. She was recommissioned on August
1, 1860, and sent to Annapolis for use by the
Naval Academy. With the start of the Civil
War, fears for her safety were raised and she
was spirited away from Annapolis on April
26, 1861, under tow to New York. The
Naval Academy was moved to Newport,
Rhode Island, and *Constitution* went along as
a training ship. After the war, in 1865,
Constitution was ordered back to Annapolis
and on that voyage was able to make better
time, under her own sail, than the tug
assigned to tow her. She was logged at thirteen and a half knots, believed to have been
her maximum speed.

Constitution began a period of inactivity
during which the duties of her commanding
officers were little more than those of ship-
keepers. One, then a lieutenant commander,
went on to great fame, as Admiral George
Dewey.

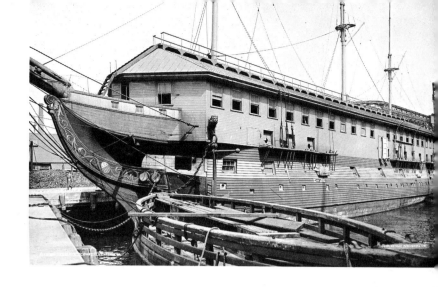

IN DOWDY GARB — *Constitution was brought to Boston in 1897 for observance of her 100th anniversary. She had been serving as a receiving ship at Portsmouth, New Hampshire. In performance of that duty, her fine lines were hidden by a barracks structure more suggestive of a farm building than anything nautical.*

The old frigate was found to be in a state of critical disrepair in 1871 and was taken to the Philadelphia Shipyard for extensive restoration. Again seaworthy, she was recommissioned in 1877 and sailed March 4, 1878, with a cargo of merchandise for exhibition at the Universal Exposition at Paris. She sailed from Le Havre on January 16, 1879, to bring home the exhibits, arriving at New York on May 24 after two mishaps: she ran aground on the English coast — the British Navy sent a warship to assist her to deep water — and had trouble with her rudder, which was repaired at Lisbon.

The next two years were spent cruising the Atlantic as a training ship for apprentices. This ended her career of sailing the high seas. She was tied up another two years at New York before being towed to Portsmouth Navy Yard as a receiving ship. John F. Fitzgerald, the maternal grandfather of President John F. Kennedy, went to Portsmouth to investigate reports that she was in danger of sinking at her pier. Fitzgerald then was a congressman from Massachusetts. An article he wrote years later reported:

I went to Portsmouth and found the facts as related in the newspaper practically true. Returning to Washington I immediately waited upon John D. Long, former Governor of Massachusetts, who was then Secretary of the Navy, and told him that unless the government did something the old frigate *Constitution* would soon be at the bottom of Portsmouth Harbor.

Mr. Long asked me to see the Chief of Construction Department, Philip Hichborn....

I told them both that the *Constitution* would celebrate the 100th anniversary of her building in the fall of 1897 and it would be a fine thing to repair the ship and bring her to Charlestown [Boston] Navy Yard, right opposite the spot where she was built 100 years before and that I would see the public authorities about having a proper celebration commemorating the event....

I presented a resolution to Congress, made a speech on the floor of the House on Jan. 14, 1897, and the ship was repaired, came to the Charlestown Navy Yard and a fine celebration, at my suggestion, by the city and State authorities, was held.... It is my belief that if this work were not done there would be no *Constitution* today.

Constitution more often came closer to destruction in the hands of her own people than through enemy action. It soon became apparent that the repairs made at Portsmouth were not sufficient, and by 1905 she was in such a sad state of disrepair it was proposed that she be taken out to sea and used as a target for the fleet.

But the public rebelled over such a fate for the gallant frigate and Congress appropriated $100,000 in 1906 for additional repairs. Thereafter she remained twenty years at her pier in the role of a museum piece, during which time she again almost hopelessly decayed.

Symbol of Sea Power

There was little official enthusiasm for financing reconstruction work needed by *Constitution* in the twenties. In 1925, Congress enacted a bill authorizing reconstruction but it provided no funds. The bill stated: "The Secretary of the Navy is . . . authorized to accept and use any donations or contributions which may be offered for the aforesaid purpose."

A nationwide campaign brought contributions of both material and cash. Children sent a deluge of small coins. But what was received fell somewhat short of what was required. The Navy Yard estimate was $650,654; much more was spent before the work was completed. Reconstruction, the most extensive until that date, slowed down or speeded up according to availability of cash and material. After it became apparent contributions would not be sufficient, Congress appropriated funds to complete the work.

On June 16, 1927, *Constitution* returned to Constitution Dry Dock, which she had christened ninety-four years earlier.

The old frigate had become so structurally weak it was feared she might literally fall apart when no longer supported by water. Wooden ships usually are hauled out at frequent intervals for cleaning, painting, and repairs below the waterline, but *Constitution* had not received this attention in many

RESCUED AGAIN — *Another urgently needed reconstruction was undertaken at the Boston Navy Yard in the 1920's. This extensive rebuilding cost more than $921,000, the bulk of which was raised by contributions of small coins by schoolchildren, public subscription, and the sale of souvenirs. Congress was called upon to furnish only $271,000 to complete the work. When* Constitution *was placed in drydock in 1927, left, extensive shoring was necessary to support her fragile hull. Decayed timber was removed and replaced with sound material. The interior of the hull also was given extensive support. Skilled wooden-ship builders were recruited wherever those members of a vanishing craft could be found, and much of the country was called upon to furnish necessary material, some of it also scarce. The stern view below is of the old warship four years later, after much of the task had been completed.*

years. Even in 1907 she was considered too fragile for drydocking. But Lieutenant John Lord, the Navy's last wooden-ship builder, so effectively supported the ancient hull within and without that there was no mishap.

Then came a quest for material, some of which became difficult to find after the passing of the wooden ship era. For masts, Douglas fir timbers, one 109 feet long, were brought on flatcars from the Pacific Northwest. *Constitution*'s original masts were of pine found in Maine, but trees of the size needed had long since been cut down. One critical item, live oak, was located in Commodore's Pond, Pensacola, Florida, where it had been stored since the 1850's, unused because iron ships supplanted wood.

Lieutenant Lord returned to Bath, Maine, where his family had been shipbuilders for generations, to look for something equally critical — shipwrights skilled in the ancient trade. He recruited some eighty of them, and he also found and borrowed the long-unused tools of the craft.

When *Constitution* was floated out of the drydock on March 16, 1930, she was as sound as the day of her 1797 launching. Repairs had cost several times her original construction cost.

Constitution left Boston under tow on July 2, 1931, after half a century of inactivity, on one of the longest voyages of her career.

Her new duty, under Commander Louis J. Gulliver, was a tour which took her to ninety ports and brought 4,614,792 visitors aboard. Although in her 134th year, she looked as though she just left her launching ways.

More than twenty-two thousand sea miles

ANCHORS AWEIGH — *Old Ironsides' sailors and marines, backs bending to the task, work capstan bars to bring the frigate's anchor aboard during a cruise that took her to ninety of the nation's ports. At right, in keeping with tradition, the crew mans her yards while getting under way. Millions of visitors who never before had an opportunity to see the famous warship came aboard at ports of call along the East, Gulf, and West Coasts. She left Boston in July 1931 and returned three years later.*

*(Editors' note: The author wrote this account of **Constitution**'s departure from Boston in 1931 for the Associated Press. It was printed in newspapers throughout the country.)*

AVAST, BELAY!

Old Ironsides Sails

By Tom Horgan

Boston, July 2 (AP) — What ship is this? U.S. Frigate **Constitution,** Sir.

Where away? Out of Boston on the afternoon tide, Sir, bound up the coast for Portsmouth, New Hampshire. Due there in the morning.

Stranger in these waters, aye, but stranger in any waters for many a year. Tied up in Boston Navy Yard since 1897, when she came home for her hundredth birthday. Came then under tow, as she is now, from Portsmouth, after some rebuilding in the Navy Yard there.

You ask why she does not cast off the tug **Grebe**'s line and break out her own white canvas? Why, bless you Sir, scarce enough men has she aboard to work her weather braces.

Of a truth, she could stand a breeze of wind, as she has often enough in the past. Time was when her scuppers, now riding so high, were rolled down to the chortling sea, but she would not mind that.

Captain Isaac Hull had a crew of 456 when he whipped the **Guerriere,** back in 1812. Now she carries but 85, and a scant 60 of those know aught of sail. She lost seven men in that engagement, and **Guerriere** 15. Not many as reckoned nowadays with rapid-fire and long-range guns,

but it was a merry go....

Aye, her sides are as stout again, and her timbers and spars as well. Lieutenant John A. Lord has seen to that. Lieutenant Lord, with 34 years' service, is the last of the Navy's wooden-ship constructors, and the shade of Joshua Humphreys who designed her, could find no fault with John Lord's work. From stem to stern no unsound bit of timber is in her hull....

Fast? Aye, that she was, and must still be, fast as sailing ships go. And that more than once kept her from destruction when beset by overpowering numbers.... Under a press of canvas she logged better than 13 knots, better speed than she's making now under tow.

ONE HAND FOR THE SHIP —
The windjammer sailor's rule of "one hand for the ship, one hand for yourself" was often ignored. Above, some of the crew are aloft in a sail-handling exercise. Spread out along a yard, they are furling one of the big square sails — and using both hands for the task. Although Constitution *carried a full suit of sail during her tour, she was towed throughout the entire trip. Constitution has not moved under sail since the nineteenth century.*

WELCOME TO NEW YORK —
Fireboats send plumes of water skyward, offering the city's traditional salute to a sea-borne visitor, as Constitution *enters New York Harbor. She was met by a marine procession of more than a hundred vessels as whistles shrieked and guns boomed.*

were traveled in three years. Commander Gulliver called it "the longest and most hazardous towing cruise in history"; it was not marred by a single accident. The towing was by U.S.S. *Grebe,* a minesweeper, which had seen service in the North Sea during World War I. The northernmost call on the Atlantic was Bar Harbor, Maine, and on the Pacific, Bellingham, Washington. Balboa, in the Canal Zone, was the southernmost.

Almost two million visitors boarded Old Ironsides in California, the greatest number from any one state. The greatest number of visitors in a single day was 36,400, at San Pedro Harbor, Los Angeles.

Constitution made Portsmouth, New Hampshire, her first port of call, and the enthusiastic reception she received was repeated throughout her entire cruise. Some thirty thousand persons came aboard in five days at Portsmouth, a town that was no stranger to Old Ironsides, for she had been repaired there in 1871 and had reported there again in 1881 as a receiving ship.

Coming down the coast, *Constitution* again called at Marblehead, Massachusetts, the little harbor that had once proved her salvation, in 1814, when it sheltered the ship from two pursuing British frigates.

Old Ironsides made many New England calls and was received with particular enthusiasm at the ancient fishing port of Gloucester, the old whaling capital of New Bedford, and Newport, Rhode Island, a town steeped in naval tradition.

Constitution was met at New York on August 29 by a nautical parade a half-mile long of more than a hundred vessels. Military planes formed another procession in the air. Gun salutes were fired ashore and afloat and whistles and sirens added to the din. Uncounted thousands lined waterfront piers and other vantage points as she proceeded to a Hudson River pier. During a two-week stay, more than a hundred thousand visitors came aboard — a figure exceeded later at Philadelphia (154,809), New Orleans (193,881), and San Pedro (478,029).

The warmth of the old frigate's welcome

AT THE GOLDEN GATE — *Old Ironsides arrived in San Francisco Bay on March 24, 1933. The Golden Gate Bridge had not yet been built, but construction had begun. Completed in 1937, the world-famous bridge spanned the place where* Constitution *is pictured. The sturdy little minesweeper* Grebe, *which towed the frigate throughout the tour, is at the extreme right.*

in the South was, in part, because the region had furnished much of her original timber and material used for repairs and rebuildings. She called at Brunswick, Georgia, passing close to St. Simons Island, from which much of the live oak used in construction was obtained.

At Port St. Joe, Florida, then a community of 851, a total of 7,479 visitors came aboard. An elderly visitor from St. Petersburg reported aboard to Commander Gulliver: "Charles Nowak, Sir. Gun captain, gun number eleven."

Nowak had served aboard nine months in 1882. The seventy-six-year-old veteran gave his old ship a close inspection and had to be persuaded *not* to climb the rigging.

After calls at Gulf ports, *Constitution* shaped a course for the Panama Canal, en route to the Pacific. She arrived at Cristobal, on the Atlantic, December 23, 1932, where almost every resident must have come aboard. Then she was cautiously towed through the "Big Ditch." She continued her triumphal tour along the West Coast, visiting almost every anchorage with sufficient water to accommodate her deep draft.

By now, the receptions had developed something of a pattern. An official welcoming delegation promptly came aboard. This was followed by representatives of various patriotic, veterans', civic, and service organizations, many with offers of cooperation and entertainment ashore for the ship's company. The ship everywhere proved a prime attraction for children.

Many residents of the Northwest felt they had a proprietary interest in the old warship. Lumbermen of the area had donated five carloads of Douglas fir for the most recent rebuilding, and the railroads had transported the timber to Boston without charge.

After reversing her course at Bellingham, Washington, *Constitution* headed back to New England, calling at some ports she had missed on the outward-bound voyage. She returned to her berth at the Boston Navy Yard on May 7, 1934, after a three-year absence to resume her station as one of the nation's historic shrines.

Preserving a Legend

Constitution returned to Boston a true national heroine. Her three-year cruise had proven to be more than an extended curtain call — it had fused both popular and official concern for her continued well-being. Amidst the gloom and despair of the Great Depression, the mere presence of the resurrected old warship gave the beleaguered nation a living symbol of continuity and renewed strength. Never again would she be allowed to drift into oblivion on the currents of neglect — the whole of America had adopted her.

For *Constitution,* the change in attitude was profound. Time and again during the course of her remarkable history, her fate had been determined by the efforts of a few stubborn individuals who each in turn had waged unrelenting campaigns to rescue the frigate from the very brink of destruction. And following each such deliverance came a rapid decline in her notoriety as the public, satisfied that the job was finished, promptly forgot her. But finally, following her 22,000-mile odyssey, she was at last clearly perceived and appreciated for what she really was: a floating national monument. Now, in the second half of her second century, she basked in the light of the popular aegis.

The Navy assumed full responsibility for Old Ironsides, according her the official status of "in service but not in commission," which was upgraded in 1941 to permanent full commission. For the better part of four decades (1940-77) she served as the flagship for the commandant of the First Naval District.

In 1954, Congress reaffirmed its dual role of benefactor-guardian of the world's oldest commissioned warship with the passage of Public Law 83-523. Signed into law by President Eisenhower, the legislation stipulated that Boston would remain *Constitution*'s permanent home port. The bill also carried the proviso that the Secretary of the Navy be empowered "to repair, equip, and restore the United States Ship *Constitution*, as far as may be practicable, to her original condition."

"Repair, equip, and restore" — it may not sound like much of a directive, but translated into real practice, it's an exacting and unending challenge for the men of *Constitution*.

Moored at her pier, guarded day and night, Old Ironsides appears safe from assault. But she's not. She's at war with the weather, an old adversary whose insidious arsenal relentlessly challenges the truth of her sobriquet. Wave action, the wind, rain, changes in temperature, and humidity — they are all continually on the attack.

It is a war of attrition, with *Constitution* sustaining all the casualties. Some years the damage is minimal; in 1977 renovations consisted of a new magazine hatch, transom waterway, and three planks in the berth deck. Other years the toll is higher, as was the case in 1970, when 50 percent of the spar deck planking had to be replaced along with the spar deck waterways and the bumkin boom. In addition, several important mast fittings and deck drains were renewed, as were the stern decorations.

Eventually, the ship must be drydocked for an overhaul. Although the actual repairs will vary, overhauls are always long and arduous affairs that require the services of wooden-ship craftsmen, of whom there are few left. And overhauls are expensive. The repair bill for *Constitution*'s 1973-75 renovation came to over $4.4 million, a figure that reflects not only the damage that the elements can create, but also the tremen-

A DATE TO REMEMBER — *The 25th anniversary of the passage of Public Law 83-523, which designated Boston as Constitution's permanent home port, was observed in 1979. Guest of honor for the occasion was former speaker for the U.S. House of Representatives John W. McCormack (lower photo) who, as a congressman from Massachusetts, was a key figure in the bill's passage. The upper photo illustrates the custom of dressing ship — flying flags from the flying jib boom up over the mastheads in an arc to the spanker boom — which is a traditional naval custom observed in honor of a special event or dignitary.*

AERIAL INSPECTION — *Hoisted aloft through a maze of running rigging, a two-man inspection team takes a close look at* Constitution's *mizzenmast. Each year a different mast is designated for a complete general refurbishing, which includes scraping and repainting of the wood surfaces and replacement as needed of the rigging. This photo provides a good example of the complex system of line (rope), block, and tackle required to manipulate large expanses of canvas. Note the authentic flag flying off the end of the spanker boom.*

dous rise in the price of materials and labor since 1797, when it cost the United States roughly one-twelfth that amount to construct the entire ship.

But no one questions the cost; history simply doesn't come cheap.

In line with standard Navy procedure, *Constitution* is now on a regularly scheduled forty-year overhaul cycle with a ten-year availability. This means that for all practical purposes she is maintained just like any other ship on the Navy list. It is her recent incorporation into "the system" that ensures that she won't fall through the slats again.

Like all ships, *Constitution* has a schedule of routine maintenance. Every day, before the visitors arrive and after they leave, her crew carries out the chores of cleaning, polishing, and general maintenance. During the long Boston winters there is usually plenty of snow to be shoveled, and when a big storm hits, the crew works round the clock to keep the decks and hatches free of snow and ice.

Coping with the elements is a job for all seasons, especially for a big wooden ship. Being painted black doesn't help. For some obscure reason (perhaps because it was the cheapest color available), black paint was the original and traditional color of paint applied to the major portion of *Constitution*'s hull. It would be hard to imagine a worse color. A lighter color naturally repels a good part of the sun's rays; black absorbs them like a sponge, causing the paint to blister and peel much more quickly. But since altering the ship's color would be an avoidable compromise to authenticity, she stays black. And

DAILY ROUTINE — Constitution's *brass shines more now than it ever did before, thanks to routine maintenance procedures for preserving all of the ship's fittings and fixtures.*

In this photo, a modern-day sailor is shown polishing a scuttle cover on the gun deck. To his right is a hatch that leads to the berth deck below, while in the background are racks of boarding cutlasses.

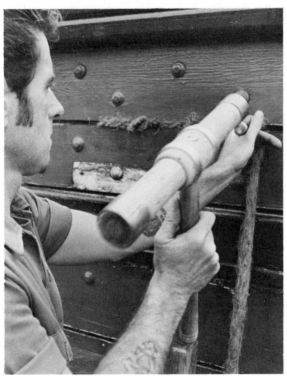

KEEPING THE WATER OUT — *The art of calking has changed little over the years. Here, a shipworker uses a combination of simple tools and deft hands to make the bulwark seams as weathertight as possible. While seawater, being briny, poses no great threat to wood, fresh water, in the form of precipitation, will rot it very quickly. As a further precaution, salt is packed between the ribs of the ship so that fresh water that manages to seep in through the sides will be transformed into a saline solution.*

AN ENDLESS TASK — *Paint, scrape, repaint* — Constitution's *crewmen find plenty of work in the form of preserving the frigate's exterior. Black paint, because it absorbs sunlight, takes merciless punishment from the sun and must be renewed at frequent intervals.*

79

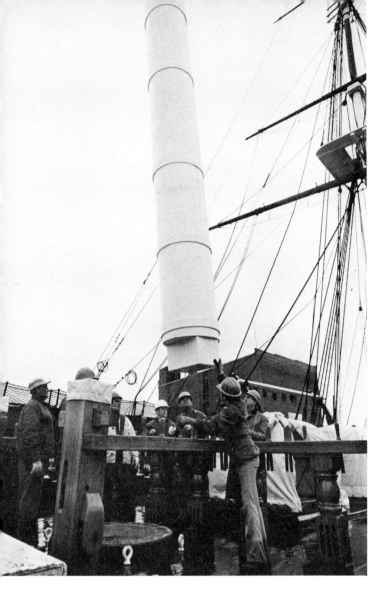

A TALL ORDER — *Restepping the mainmast is a critical maneuver, even with the use of modern equipment. The left photo shows the main section of the mast being raised by two cranes. A few careful moments later (above photo), it has been swung into a vertical position above the spar deck where experienced hands will guide it below to the mast step, a stout structure affixed to the keelson. The photo clearly shows how the heel of the mast is tenoned so that, when it rests in the mortised step, the mast cannot twist in the wind. This restepping took place on a wet morning in the fall of 1979.*

to keep her painted and presentable, the Navy scrapes, sands, and repaints the exterior hull every two years.

Constitution's masts are restored on a rotating basis. Taking in turn the bowsprit, foremast, mainmast, and mizzenmast, repair crews annually tackle one of the towering spars and all of its yards. The finish is first stripped away right down to bare wood, which permits a careful inspection for structural damage that may have occurred during the preceding three years. It is then repainted, the mast white and the yards black.

There comes a time in every mast's life, however, when it becomes so fatigued by the motion of wind and wave that it must be unshipped and either rebuilt or replaced. Though the task of removing and restepping masts has been made much smoother by the use of modern cranes, it is still a major undertaking, and everyone breathes a lot easier when the job is done. Just prior to the lowering of the great mast, an ancient ceremony takes place deep within the bowels of the ship at the mast step, a heavy oak mortice into which the squared "heel" or "foot" of the mast is anchored. The ritual consists of placing a number of coins in the bottom of the step, after which the mast is eased down into position and secured. Pinned in place by several tons of wood, the coins supposedly bring good luck to the ship. Sailors have always taken their superstitions seriously, and the coin ritual is practiced as religiously in the twentieth century as it was in the eighteenth.

Each September, the entire ship is inspected in detail to pinpoint any structural deterioration that may have come about during the preceding year. The findings derived from this truck-to-keel physical are then evaluated during a work-planning conference. At the conference, Navy officials establish just which repairs should receive priority attention during the coming months and an appropriate work schedule is mapped out.

The threat of fire is ever present for a

wooden vessel. In the interest of keeping that danger to a minimum, the Navy has outfitted *Constitution* with modern fire safety apparatus, including a complete sprinkler system. Purists may decry the existence of such things, demanding strict adherence to historically correct detail, right down to the flickering whale-oil lamps that once provided token illumination for the dim recesses below decks. But the line between stainless authenticity and common sense must be drawn — some risks to life and property are just too great to be ignored.

There are other modern concessions, such as electric lights, a quarterdeck shack, and hot-air heating. Such "anachronisms" are designed to be as unobstrusive as possible, and actually they detract little from the historically intense atmosphere one feels when touring the ship.

Constitution's "total fitness program" takes many forms, including the famous "turnaround," which occurs annually on the Fourth of July. The maneuver has become what is surely Boston's most famous nautical event. Its primary function is to literally turn the ship around 180 degrees each year so that she alternately presents her port and starboard side to the weather. The theory behind this is that the vessel will eventually warp and weather unevenly if she is moored in the same position indefinitely.

The turnaround is a gala happening, probably unique in the world. With an entourage of invited guests clustered along the length of her spar deck, the stately old warrior slowly eases away from her berth, a tugboat on each side. Then, with all the pomp and ceremony befitting her age and station, she is squired around Boston Harbor. The "cruise" is brief, but for a few triumphant moments time looks the other way as the Eagle of the Sea returns to her element.

An occasional excursion is also taken in conjunction with important occasions of state — as in 1975-76 — during America's Bicentennial. In the summer of 1976, when the "Tall Ships," a flotilla of international sailing vessels, called at New York and Boston, there was no question that *Constitution* would carry the official local welcoming party. On a brilliant July afternoon the indomitable old frigate, assisted by her two tugs, made way out to Castle Island at the mouth of Boston Harbor to greet the windjammers and lead them into port in a breathtaking "parade of sail."

The following day she was called upon to take part in the visit to the United States of the reigning British monarch, Queen Elizabeth II. Examined in historical perspective, the event was ironic. Here was the United States, wildly celebrating the 200th anniversary of its declaration of independence from Great Britain, being paid a call by the present-day counterpart of old King George

ONE GOOD TURN — *With Boston's modern skyline gliding by in stark contrast to her wooden spars,* Constitution *completes her annual turnaround, accompanied on the brief cruise by an unofficial convoy of civilian craft. Carried out annually on the Fourth of July, the turnaround's basic purpose is to equalize the ship's exposure to the elements by rotating her pierside position 180 degrees to avoid warpage and uneven weathering of the ship's structure. The turnaround of the ancient frigate has become a colorful and eagerly anticipated event of Boston's summer season.*

Effective July 4, 1979, Constitution *was ordered by a new Naval directive to render the official 21-gun National Salute "while underway" on her annual turnaround.*

INSURANCE — *In the event of fire aboard ship, only immediate action would save* Constitution *from going up in flame and smoke. In the interest of safety, a few modern devices, such as this fire alarm, have been installed.*

ROYAL VISITOR ABOARD —
For the first time in her history,
Constitution *hosted a British monarch in 1976, when Queen Elizabeth II was in America to wish the country well during its Bicentennial festivities. In a brief ceremony held in the captain's cabin, the queen was presented with an exquisite small sea chest made from live oak salvaged during a recent overhaul of* Constitution. *The chest was created in nearby Arlington, Massachusetts by The Old Schwamb Mill and is lined with deerskin. On the right is J. William Middendorf II, then Secretary of the Navy, who made the presentation. The queen's visit underscored the strong bond that has developed between the two countries in the years since the Revolutionary War and the War of 1812.*

LEADING THE WAY — *One of the stellar events of the United States Bicentennial in 1976 was the appearance of the "Tall Ships," their towering spars and vast expanses of sail thrilling thousands of spectators who watched in person and millions more who watched on television. When the great white armada of 64 vessels visited Boston,* Constitution *was dispatched to greet and lead the awesome "parade of sail" through Boston harbor. Photo shows the frigate firing a salute. In the background is a three-masted schooner, one of the many modern vessels who "inherited the wind" from Old Ironsides. The "Tall Ships" returned in 1980 with* Constitution *repeating her role of four years earlier.*

himself. The incongruity was further heightened by the presentation of an extraordinary gift to Her Majesty during her visit to *Constitution*. Shortly after *Constitution* had rendezvoused with H.M.Y. *Britannia* and the queen had come aboard Old Ironsides for a VIP tour, she was escorted below to the captain's cabin. There Secretary of the Navy J. William Middendorf II presented her with an exquisitely executed sea chest made from live oak salvaged during a recent overhaul of *Constitution*. Undoubtedly many of the queen's royal ancestors would have liked to have seen the whole ship "in a box"! This unique presentation, and the whole of the queen's visit, served to illustrate the high regard that the two countries have for each other.

The mid-seventies witnessed cutbacks in military spending, which resulted in the Navy's abandonment of several shipyards, including the one in Boston. For a time it appeared that *Constitution* might be forced to seek a new home port. Offers of berthage were received from several other naval installations. But in an unusually fortunate turn of events, the Boston Naval Shipyard was acquired by the National Park Service, which subsequently rented all the necessary facilities back to the Navy, allowing the First Naval District to leave *Constitution* in Boston, her traditional home port, where unanimous popular opinion felt she belonged.

In the words of an official United States Navy history: *Constitution* remains in commission today, the oldest ship on the Navy List, [a] proud and worthy representative of the Navy's great days of fighting sail, and [a] symbol of the courage and patriotic service of generations of Americans at sea where much of the Nation's destiny will always lie."

Vitally maintained, nationally venerated, and respected around the world, *Constitution* occupies an unrivaled post in America's seafaring annals. She rests today in eloquent silence, her holds heavy with heritage, her masts still reaching for glory.

late Rear Admiral Samuel Eliot Morison, perhaps the country's most important naval historian and one of *Constitution*'s greatest friends, the library makes its resources available to scholars of history as well as the general public. Its information pool is also the nucleus for illustrated talks and lectures that the museum presents to civic groups and schools.

Other educational programs offered by the museum include guided tours, workshops in marine crafts, the preparation and dispersal of classroom materials, and the Samuel Eliot Morison Lecture Series.

To maintain its facilities and services, the museum must devote considerable effort to fund raising. In addition to monies derived from sales at its museum store, the institution receives funding from a growing base of support in both the private and business sectors. Currently, the museum has a membership of about 2000 individuals and corporations, representing forty states and five foreign countries. Annual dues from these members comprise a significant portion of the museum's operating budget.

Similar enthusiasm for the venture is

MEMORABILIA — *Young couple pauses before an arresting display of artifacts on the museum's main floor. Each year the institution welcomes more than 100,000 visitors.*

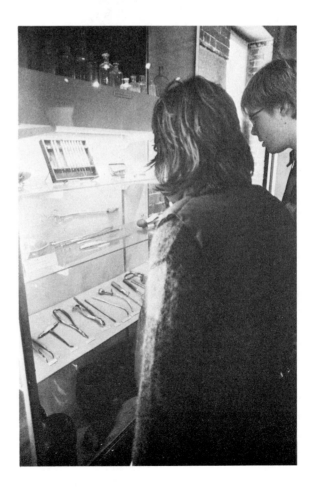

A SHIP'S BOATS — *In the days of sail, a ship carried numerous small boats that performed many tasks.* Constitution *customarily carried about eight such launches, including this wherry now on display in the museum. On board the ship, three boats of successively shorter lengths were nested one inside the other, to conserve space, on the spar deck hatch. The various small boats performed multiple duties. They assisted in docking the ship by carrying out lines to the pier; they transported supplies and messages between ship and shore; and, of course, they had the pleasant chore of carrying liberty parties ashore.*

PRECISE MODEL — *The museum houses several replicas of* Constitution, *including this fine example of the model maker's art. Unerring attention to detail and scale gives this replica a high degree of authenticity.*

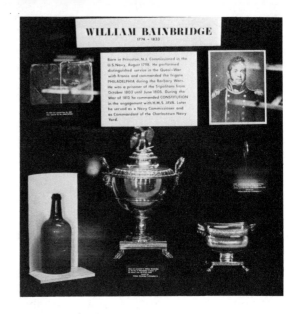

being expressed through the donation of historical items and documents related to Old Ironsides. The idea of such an institution has prompted many people to come forward with these artifacts in the interest of sharing such treasures with the public at large in a safe and appropriate setting.

Open daily except Thanksgiving, Christmas, and New Year's Day, the U.S.S. *Constitution* Museum annually attracts over 100,000 visitors who take advantage of its displays and learning exhibits. In a sense, the museum picks up where the tour of the ship leaves off, amplifying many aspects of *Constitution*'s career at sea and further enriching the public's appreciation of our nation's naval history.

EARLY WAGES — *This interesting chart illustrates the pay scale established by the Navy in 1798. While it is true that a dollar went much further back then, it is probably safe to assume that America's early sailors were not grossly overpaid!*

A NAVAL HERO — *William Bainbridge commanded* Constitution *when she defeated* Java *during the War of 1812. Although twice wounded during this engagement, Bainbridge stayed on deck directing the action until victory was secured. One officer aboard* Java *later remarked admiringly that* Constitution *was handled so skillfully "it made me regret that she was not British." This museum display recalls some of the highlights of Bainbridge's distinguished career.*

Complement of men and their monthly salaries, set by the Navy Department in 1798.

Commander	1	$75	Yeoman of gun-room	1	$13
Lieutenants	4	40	Gunner	1	18
Lieutenants of Marines	2	26	Quarter Gunners	11	13
Sailing Masters	2	40	Coxswain	1	13
Master's Mates	2	20	Sailmaker	1	18
Midshipmen	7	19	Cooper	1	13
Purser	1	40	Steward	1	13
Surgeon	1	50	Armorer	1	13
Surgeon's Mates	2	30	Master at arms	1	13
Clerk	1	25	Cook	1	13
Carpenter	1	18	Chaplain	1	40
Carpenter's Mates	2	13	Able Seamen	120	11
Boatswain	1	18	Ordinary Seamen	150	9
Boatswain's Mates	2	13	Boys	30	8
Marines, including sergeants and corporals				50	
				400	

This number was increased to nearly **500 men** when carronades were added.

Epilogue

The combined effects of time, the elements, and the enemy were particularly harsh on wooden warships. Few survived beyond the age of thirty. That *Constitution* is not only still afloat but in better shape than ever before clearly demonstrates that she is perceived as much more than a mere ship made of wood, metal, rope, and glass. There is something more. You can't see it or touch it, but it is there, an aura that tarries forever in the footsteps of long-dead heroes. Call it spirit if you will, but it transcends that definition. History has rewarded Old Ironsides' unstinting loyalty by granting her a soul, a soul born of fire, blood, and sacrifice.

It is well that past generations have preserved *Constitution,* and it is imperative that we and those who follow us do no less. She's an enduring symbol of our nation's struggle to prevail in a world that has always contained those who threaten the existence of liberty and freedom — a struggle that continues to this day. We are the keepers of the flame that forged a nation, and as such it is incumbent upon us to preserve this valiant old vessel, which embodies the very essence of our nation's intrepid spirit.

By so doing, we draw close to the truth that is America.

INDEX

Illustration credits

Most of the photographs in this volume are the work of Peter Vandermark, photographer of Charlestown, Massachusetts.

Other illustration credits are as follows:
Frank B. Denman, 102
John F. Kennedy Memorial Library, 10
Library of Congress, 29, 34-35, 42(top), 58, 60, 61, 63, 65-67, 70-71
U.S. Navy, Mariners Museum, Newport News, Virginia, 32
National Archives, 22

Naval Photographic Center (painting by Gerhard Geidel), 124-125
New England Mutual Life Insurance Company, 25
The New York Historical Society, New York City, 53
Tom Jones, 84
U.S. Marine Corps, 40, 41
U.S. Navy, 6, 12, 21, 23, 27, 30, 36-37, 39, 42, 44-45, 47-51, 54-55, 57, 64, 68, 69, 93-95, 82-83, 85, 98, 119, 126